GIFTS FROM THE HEART

In front of her was a boy Torie didn't know—although she had noticed him around school. How could she not notice a guy like that? He was absolutely *gorgeous*!

The boy's hair was thick and black, brushed straight back, and he had a lean, chiseled face with deep-set dark eyes and high cheekbones. But the thing about this boy that Torie had noticed most of all had nothing to do with his looks. Torie could sense how restless he was from clear across the room. He exuded a pent-up energy, like an animal in a cage.

Torie looked around the room at all the students with their noses in their work—all except the boy in front. Turning back to him she saw he had his head cocked back and was ruffling up the back of his hair, while looking straight at her with those deep, dark eyes.

Gifts From The Heart

Joanne Simbal

BANTAM BOOKS
TORONTO • NEW YORK • LONDON • SYDNEY • AUCKLAND

To David Hajdu

RL 6, IL age 11 and up

GIFTS FROM THE HEART
A Bantam Book / June 1988

Cover photo by Pat Hill

ISBN 0-553-27228-4

Published simultaneously in the United States and Canada

Bantam Books are published by Bantam Books, a division of Bantam Doubleday Dell Publishing Group, Inc. Its trademark, consisting of the words "Bantam Books" and the portrayal of a rooster, is Registered in U.S. Patent and Trademark Office and in other countries. Marca Registrada. Bantam Books, 666 Fifth Avenue, New York, New York 10103.

PRINTED IN THE UNITED STATES OF AMERICA

O   0 9 8 7 6 5 4 3 2 1

Chapter One

The party stopped. The dancers froze. The band held a single note until it faded into the still and silent ballroom. But she didn't care. She never cared what anyone ever thought. She always did exactly what she wanted, whenever she wanted.

Torie Hilliard stared at her words on the paper but couldn't get her voice to work. Everyone in the class had had to stand up and read his or her story aloud. She hated reading in front of the class, especially when she was supposed to read something she had written herself.

It took about ten seconds, and it seemed like ten *hours*, but Torie's English teacher finally got the message. "All right, Victoria," said Mr. Moyer. "I'll hear your story another time—that is, after school. See me this afternoon, in room four-oh-two."

That's just great, thought Torie as she took her seat.

After class Torie hurried off to meet her two best friends, Joanne Carey and Wendy Burnett. Jo and Torie had been best friends since the fourth grade.

Both of the girls were pretty. Torie was small boned and fair, with wavy, long brown hair and brown eyes. Joe was a couple of inches taller and quite a bit rounder.

During their freshman year Wendy had moved in next door to Jo, and the three girls had become almost inseparable. They always met at Jo's locker after fourth period on their way to lunch. That day, Torie got there first.

"Hey, Joey," she called out as she saw her best friend approach.

Jo stopped for an instant. Nobody, except Torie, ever referred to her as "Joey" anymore. Even Torie reserved the name for times when she had something personal to talk about. "Joey," Torie said, "I'm sorry, but I have to cancel for this afternoon. I can't go."

"But Mitch is bringing a date for you," Jo said. "Some new guy on the soccer team."

Jo had a boyfriend: Mitch Delaney, the tall, blond forward on the varsity soccer team. That had become the big difference between the girls now that they both were juniors.

Torie sighed as she thought about the dates she'd had. She had gone out with half a dozen guys over the past couple of years, all of whom were nice enough and fairly good-looking, yet Torie never seemed to want to go out with anyone more than once or twice. She hadn't been able to find anyone special. Torie had never been in love.

And this wasn't going to be the day for it, the way Torie saw things. "I'm sorry. I really want to go. But I can't," said Torie.

Jo looked at her with concern. "Why, what happened, Torie?"

As they hustled down the halls, Torie explained, "It's so stupid. I feel like an absolute goof. I was in English, and I was supposed to read in front of the class, and I just couldn't. I guess I was embarrassed. Now I feel *twice* as embarrassed, because I made a jerk of myself.

"Anyway," Torie said, continuing, "Mr. Moyer wants me to read my story after school." The girls walked into the cafeteria, found three chairs together, and took their lunches out of their bags. "So I have to do it today. I have to go to see Mr. Moyer in room four-oh-two."

"That's detention hall," said Jo.

"I know. Isn't it wonderful?" Torie asked sarcastically. "Mr. Moyer happens to have detention duty, so I have to go and read my story in front of the entire detention hall. And you'll be out with Mitch—and whoever-he-is on the soccer team!"

"Now, now, don't worry," came a voice from behind Torie and Jo. "I'll take care of everything!"

"Wendy," said Torie, "where'd you come from?"

"I was walking right behind you the whole time. I heard the whole story," said Wendy, sitting down next to Torie. "But not to worry, girls. Wendy Burnett to the rescue. I will gladly take your date, Tor."

"Thanks a lot," Torie said. "You're all heart."

"No problem." Wendy cheerfully dug her spoon into a dish of ice cream. She firmly believed that if she skipped the main course, dessert couldn't possibly be fattening.

Torie studied her friend, wondering how she got away with so much. Funny and outgoing, Wendy was probably more popular than either Torie or Jo. Even though she could get a little too sarcastic and she wasn't exactly gorgeous, Wendy seemed to get invited to every party and had gone out with just about every good-looking boy at Arlenton.

4

"So," Wendy said, turning to Jo and flipping her hair over her shoulder with a dramatic gesture. "What color are his eyes, and how do you think he feels about striking redheads?"

Torie moaned and buried her head in her arms.

"Wendy," Jo said fiercely, "you're not helping."

Wendy patted Torie's arm sympathetically. "I'm sorry," she said. "I was only teasing. I promise you I won't even look at the guy."

"It doesn't matter," Torie said, sitting up with a sigh. "I just wish I could get out of going to room four-oh-two."

Later that afternoon as the last bell of the day rang, Torie gathered her books together and forced herself toward Room 402. Room 402 wasn't just a number at Arlenton High. It meant something like the term "Sing-Sing" in the old gangster movies. Detention hall was hardly Torie's idea of a great after-school social atmosphere.

She poked her head partway into the room, peering around the door frame. There were about a dozen students at desks, diligently writing detention assignments. At the head of the room, Mr. Moyer was sitting at the teacher's desk deliberately rubbing his hands together in slow motion.

In front of him, facing him, was a boy Torie didn't know—although she had noticed him around school. How could she not notice a guy like that? He was absolutely *gorgeous*!

The boy's hair was thick and black, brushed straight back, and he had a lean, chiseled face with deep-set dark eyes and high cheekbones. His skin was tanned, Torie noticed, unusually tanned for so early in the season. He was wearing black leather boots, a deep blue cotton sweatshirt, and well-worn black denim jeans.

But the thing about this boy that Torie had noticed most of all had nothing to do with his looks. It was the way he carried himself and the way he moved. He stood straight backed and tall, but he never stood still. He would constantly shift the weight of his body from one side to the other, peer around the room, and ruffle the back of his hair with the palm of his hand. Torie could sense how restless he was from clear across the room. He exuded a pent-up energy, like an animal in a cage.

"Now," said Mr. Moyer, "Kyle Fontana."

Torie ran his name through her mind. Something about it sounded familiar, but she couldn't pinpoint what it was.

"Yesterday afternoon," the teacher said, "as

I understand, you walked up to another student, Brian Howser, and proceeded to sock him in the jaw. Unfortunately, Howser hasn't shown up for class since. But we caught you."

Oh, no, Torie told herself. *Just when I get interested in a guy, he turns out to be some troublemaker.*

"That's not the way it happened," said Kyle.

"No?" asked Mr. Moyer. "Then why don't you tell me the whole story."

There was silence. Neither Kyle Fontana nor the teacher blinked an eye.

"Listen," said the teacher. "You're not helping yourself. I want an answer, or I'm going to be twice as hard on you."

Silence again.

"All right, Fontana. You've dug your own grave now. Sit down in front of me—now!"

Kyle took a seat in silence, and Torie took a long, deep breath. "Excuse me," she said, tapping on the doorframe.

"Oh—Victoria," said Mr. Moyer. "Come in. And let me see your story. I'd like to see what it is that you don't want anyone to hear."

Without a sound, Torie handed over her notebook and waited while her teacher read from it silently. Torie sighed, relieved that he wasn't asking her to read it to him.

Finally Mr. Moyer said, "I've got to tell you

that this is quite good. I have no idea why you wouldn't be proud to read this in class. This passage, for instance—

" 'She headed off alone into the northern autumn mídnight, the moon a single step behind her, like the fear she just broke free from.' "

"Please," Torie interrupted, red faced with embarrassment. "Don't read any more. Not out loud."

"Don't worry," said Mr. Moyer. "I assure you, nobody here is very interested in literature."

Torie looked around the room at all the other students with their noses in their work—all except Kyle Fontana. He had his head cocked back, he was ruffling up the back of his hair again, and he was looking straight at Torie with those deep, dark eyes.

Chapter Two

The next morning, just as the bell rang to start her study hall, Torie gave Jo a gentle kick under the long table where they were sitting. Kyle Fontana was almost running into the room. Had he been in her study hall all along? Torie wondered.

"Pssst, Jo," Torie whispered across the study hall table. "Take a look at that guy who just came in. You know anything about him?"

"Nope," Jo whispered back. "But let's check him out. Watch where he sits, and we'll see what kind of crowd he's in."

Kyle wasn't hard to watch. "Excuse me," he said out loud as he took one of the few remaining empty seats. It was right next to Jo.

Torie darted her eyes down at her note pad,

on which she was already doodling. *Now be cool,* she told herself. *Be cool.* She opened her history book and pretended to be interested in the Monroe Doctrine. Torie had read the same paragraph about five times when, suddenly, Kyle reached across the table and tapped her hand.

With a start, Torie pulled her hand away from Kyle and stared up at him in surprise. He was leaning across the table toward her, with a cute, sort-of-cocky smile.

"About the moon—" said Kyle. "If it's autumn, and you're in the north, and it's midnight, the moon wouldn't be behind you. It would be traveling in a really low, really long arc across the western sky."

His voice dropped to a whisper. "It's a pretty sight," he said. "As pretty as the story you wrote."

Torie looked straight down at her book and tried to let this sink in for a second. *What's this guy's story?* she asked herself. *Whatever it is, he sure doesn't have a confidence problem!*

Obviously, Torie realized, he had been listening to her story the day before in detention hall—listening very closely. And he remembered every word.

"Young man!" barked Mr. Robb, the teacher

monitoring study hall. "This is a study hall, not a social event. Over here, please." And before Torie could do or say anything at all, Kyle had walked over to a table by Mr. Robb, where he spent the rest of the study hall.

Later Torie didn't go to the cafeteria but decided to spend her lunch period in the school library. It was one of her favorite places; Torie felt as if she *belonged* in this quiet space where the books she loved came alive for her. It didn't take her long to find what she was looking for—a book about astronomy.

That evening, alone at home, Torie settled in to read. Her bedroom was made for reading, she believed. It was a big, bright room with built-in bookshelves on the second floor of a house Torie's dad always called "prewar," though which war, nobody knew. She knew there weren't many other houses like hers left in Arlenton, her hometown in the hills of northeast Pennsylvania. Long ago, Torie's house had been a farmhouse. Then the interstate highway came through, the housing developments were built, and everything was changed. Or *almost* everything. A few miles from her bedroom window, Torie could still see the last farms outside the Arlenton town line.

The moon that lit the farms that night reminded Torie of Kyle, and it reminded her to go through that astronomy book to see what he had been talking about in study hall. She plowed through half the book until she found the section about "lunar trajectory." Most of it was too technical for Torie, but she read very closely and sure enough, it said almost exactly the same thing Kyle had told her.

Now Torie was sort of confused about Kyle. Judging by what she knew about astronomy, he was obviously pretty smart. And from the time she saw him in detention hall, Torie knew Kyle was very different from most of the boys she knew. Then again, Torie remembered *why* Kyle was in detention hall. If he was the kind of guy who was always getting into fights, then he might just be more than she wanted to handle.

Torie shut the astronomy book and tried to convince herself to stop thinking about Kyle Fontana and concentrate on her writing instead. Just about every night for the past year, she had set aside time to write. The four notebooks filled with her stories were proof of her secret dream to someday be a writer. She took out the unfinished story she had shown Mr. Moyer. The English teacher had made her promise that she'd let him see more of it. Torie stared at the story for a moment. Maybe on paper she always said and did exactly what she wanted, but she had a feeling that in real life the only person that fit that description was Kyle Fontana.

Two days later Torie had added six pages to her story. Hesitantly, she approached Mr. Moyer at the end of class.

"You wanted to see more of my story," she said, offering the pages to him.

"I'm glad you brought it," Mr. Moyer replied. "But I don't have time to look at it right now. Do you think you could bring it to Room four-oh-two this afternoon?"

"Sure," Torie said, this time not feeling quite so bad about Room 402. She wondered if Kyle would be there.

But later that afternoon, when Torie looked into Room 402, Kyle wasn't there. Brian Howser was.

Torie watched it all from out in the hall. Howser sat slumped low in his seat, staring defiantly at the ceiling. Mr. Moyer stood over him with his arms folded, and between them was a pale, small-framed boy who looked as if he were a junior high school student. He was clutching a backpack against his chest.

"That's the whole story," said the smaller boy. "Brian tried to take my pack away from me, and when I held on to it, he started hitting me. That's when the other guy came."

"Kyle Fontana?" asked Mr. Moyer.

Torie listened closely, fascinated.

"I guess so. I never saw him before," said the younger boy. "He came out of this old gray Jeep, and he helped me, and I grabbed my bag, and I got away as fast as I could."

"Well, I'll be . . ." muttered Mr. Moyer. "He never said . . ."

That's what really happened, Torie realized. Kyle was actually trying to help a smaller guy, someone he didn't even know! To top it off, he'd taken detention, rather than embarrass the kid.

Thoughtfully, Torie turned around and headed home. Mr. Moyer would have to read her story another time. Right then Torie could only think of one thing—Kyle. And she kept thinking about him all through the night.

The next day was fabulously beautiful. As a result, Arlenton High students were allowed to spend some time outdoors after eating lunch, until the next period began. Everybody in the school seemed to be out on the school grounds, including Torie, Jo, and Wendy. The girls were curled up under a tree

14

where they could look out over the entire stretch of grounds.

Jo and Wendy were talking about a sale at their favorite store, but Torie was quieter than usual. Though she was making a halfhearted effort to follow their conversation, she was actually making a careful survey of the school grounds.

Finally Torie spotted him. Shading her eyes with the sides of both hands, Torie squinted into the sun. She could see Kyle in silhouette, walking along the grass on the other side of the grounds. Soon he stopped and leaned up against a big old tree.

"Hey, look over there," Torie said. "Way over, almost by the parking lot. See that guy with the black hair leaning against the tree?"

"Where?" asked Jo, squinting in the same direction as Torie.

"Way over— Ooh!" said Torie. "He disappeared!" Grabbing a notebook to shade her eyes better, Torie looked a little harder. "Okay—there!" she said. "Now he's over to the left, sitting on the grass. See?"

"Well—no," said Jo. "Where?"

Now Wendy was trying to find him, too. But refusing to squint, she put on sunglasses.

"He moved again!" said Torie. "Why can't he stand still for one minute?"

"Torie, dear, what are we looking for?" asked Wendy. "A boy—or a frog?"

Laughing a little, despite herself, Torie turned to her friend. "Very funny, very funny."

"Hold on," Jo interrupted. "Tor, you looking for that guy from study hall?"

"Well, yeah—why?" answered Torie.

"Isn't that him?" said Jo, pointing toward the road in front of the school. Sure enough, there was Kyle, zipping down the road in a Jeep. He had the top down, and he had taken his shirt off. As he passed by, the bright noon sunlight glistened off the muscles of his dark, tanned shoulders.

Torie stood up and watched him intently. Behind her, both of the other girls got up, too.

"Not bad," said Wendy.

"Uh-huh," Jo agreed. "You know, he looks better than he looked in study hall."

Torie turned to Jo and grinned. "In study hall, he had all his clothes on," she said. "What I can't figure out is why I never noticed him in our study hall before."

"That's easy," Jo replied. "You never noticed him before, because he never bothered to show up."

"I hate to change the subject," Wendy said, "but sixth period's going to start pretty soon. We'd better go back inside."

The girls headed toward the main entrance to school, along with the rest of the lunch-time crowd. As they walked along Wendy turned to Torie. "Well," she demanded, "who is that guy, anyway? You know him?"

"Not really. His name's Kyle Fontana," answered Torie, looking straight ahead. "Ever hear of him?"

"Nope. But I'll tell you one thing I know."

"What?" asked Torie.

"He's in a lot of trouble," answered Wendy.

"Why?" asked Torie, slowing down her pace.

"You can't just disappear in the middle of the school day like that!" answered Wendy. "The next period is going to start in five minutes."

"Oh—that's right," said Torie. "I wonder where . . ."

Soon, the three girls were in the middle of the thick crowd of students being herded back into school. Lost in thought, Torie fell behind Jo and Wendy and ended up at the tail end of the crowd.

Suddenly Torie was startled by the sound of somebody opening a bottle directly behind her. She turned around quickly. It was Kyle, with his shirt back on, taking a drink from a bottle of cola.

As soon as Torie saw him, she abruptly

17

turned around again. *How did he get here so soon?* she wondered. *He sure moves fast!*

"Oh, it's you—the writer," said Kyle, maneuvering his way alongside Torie as they walked into school together. "Hi! Want some soda?"

"No thanks," answered Torie, nervously turning her head to face him. He smiled at her, and she felt a little better—and a little more nervous at the same time. They walked inside the building side by side and stopped together in the front hall.

"Are you sure you don't want some soda?" asked Kyle. "I just bought it a minute ago. It's good and cold—just what you need on a day like this." He leaned back against the wall, taking a drink from the bottle.

Torie stood straight in front of Kyle, holding her books and purse in front of her with both arms. "I can't believe you," she said, truly surprised at his cool, defiant attitude. "Did you bring a hamburger in here, too?"

"Sorry," said Kyle with a grin. "I would have if I knew you were hungry."

He started to laugh, and Torie joined in, suddenly feeling much more comfortable.

"Isn't it against the rules to have a soda in school?" Torie asked as she looked up at Kyle.

Kyle shrugged his shoulders. "I don't know," he said. "Why would it be?"

"I don't know, but since Arlenton's got more rules than any other high school in the state, I think you'd better be careful, anyway." She looked around nervously only to see Mr. Robb heading straight toward them. Luckily, it seemed as if he hadn't noticed them yet. "Here, let me have that for a minute," Torie said, taking Kyle's bottle of soda.

Kyle smiled down at her. "I knew you were thirsty."

"I'm not thirsty," Torie said as she slipped the half-full bottle into her purse. "I'm just trying to hide this thing for you!"

Just then, Mr. Robb walked up to the two of them. They didn't budge, and the teacher kept on walking, without saying a word.

When the coast was clear, Torie adjusted her books to start walking to class. "I'd better get to history," she said, "or I'll be late."

Kyle pushed himself away from the wall. "Wait a minute," he said. "What are you going to do with that soda? Are you going to carry it around in your purse?"

Torie stopped to think about it.

"If you do that," said Kyle, "It'll get your papers and stuff all messed up. Here, I'll take it."

"If you do that, it'll get you another deten-tion pass," said Torie, backing away from Kyle.

"Hold it, Victoria," he said.

She stopped. *He remembered my name*, she realized.

"Here," he said, "I have something for you." Without letting Torie see what it was, Kyle slipped something into her hand. It was just a bottle cap, Torie realized, but after he tucked it into the palm of her hand, he kept her hand in his and held it gently but firmly.

"Thanks for the help," said Kyle and he let go of her hand.

"Okay, *Kyle*," said Torie softly, and she turned and rushed off down the hall to her class.

Chapter Three

Maybe it wasn't the most mature decision she had ever made in her life, but Torie felt like keeping the soda bottle she had gotten from Kyle. Of course it was just a soda bottle, and she knew it. Still, she emptied it out, brought it home, and put it on top of her desk.

Every night after school, while Torie was working on her story, the empty bottle reminded her of Kyle. Unfortunately, that was *all* Torie had to remind her of Kyle. Three days and three nights passed, and they hadn't talked to each other again.

Torie spotted him around school, but he was always far off in the distance. He was always alone, and he always seemed to be in such a hurry. *This guy is so mysterious,* Torie thought, though that only made him more exciting to her.

She tried to keep her head together by focusing on her writing. But Kyle was even influencing Torie's story. On Thursday night she started rewriting the passage about the moon that Kyle had corrected when he first spoke to her in study hall.

Flipping through the pages of her story, Torie found the section she was looking for. She ripped it out of her notebook, crumbled it into a ball, and tossed it into the white wicker basket she kept beside the desk in her bedroom.

"So long, northern autumn moon," she mumbled under her breath. "Now—what did he say, *exactly*?"

Torie closed her eyes and conjured up a mental picture of that moment with Kyle in study hall. She saw him again, just as he had been then. And as he started talking to Torie, in her mind, she wrote down every word.

"About the moon . . ."

Torie wrote fast, her eyes half-closed. In a minute she had it all down.

"It's a pretty sight. As pretty as the story you wrote. As pretty as you look to me, Torie . . ."

"Slow down!" Torie said out loud, realizing that she had started to write down quite a bit more than Kyle had actually said.

Slapping her notebook closed, Torie got up from her desk, sat on her bed, and grabbed the phone from her night table.

"Joey," she said, while Jo's number was still ringing. "Be home tonight."

When her best friend answered, Torie lay back flat on her bed. "Hi ya," she began, "want to talk about astronomy?"

"Hi, Tor," answered Jo. "What are you talking about?"

"The problem is what I'm *thinking* about," said Torie. "I'm here trying to write, and I can't. I keep thinking about that guy."

"Who?" said Jo. "That guy from study hall—Mr. Mystery Man?"

"Uh-huh," answered Torie. "You know, I think maybe he's *too* mysterious for me. I haven't seen him or heard a word from him in days. Now, I don't know what to think. I don't even really know what kind of guy he is. Maybe he's a total wild man. I don't know."

"Okay, okay," said Jo. "Let's get a grip, huh?"

"Easy for you to say," answered Torie.

"Listen," said Jo. "Let's start from the beginning. Now, you don't really know anything about this guy. Right?"

"Well, I know a *little*," said Torie.

"Like what?" asked Jo.

"Like—I think I'm crazy about him," said Torie, and both girls started to laugh.

"What more do you need to know?" said Jo. "But, if you want to get to know this guy, you're going to have to do something about it. You can't just sit there. Go after him."

"Come on, Jo. I can't do that," said Torie. "You know me. I need *him* to come after *me*. But only the goofs seem to come up to me."

"You and every other girl," said Jo. "It's only in the movies or books that guys like that go after the girl."

Torie stopped and thought for a second. "Maybe you're right, Jo," she said. "All right. Thanks. Hey, what are you doing tomorrow? You seeing Mitch?"

"Yeah, I'm going to soccer practice to watch him play," said Jo.

"Okay," said Torie. "See you later, then."

"Good luck, Tor," said Jo.

Springing up from her bed, Torie swung

her desk chair over to the bookcase next to her window. "Maybe you have a point, Jo," she said. "The guys *do* go after the girl in books."

Torie ran her eyes over the shelves until she found three of her favorite books. "Okay, girls," Torie said, settling them in a pile on her desk. "Let's see how *you* got *your* guys. Whatever you did, if it's good enough for the most gorgeous guys in history, it's good enough for Kyle Fontana."

Torie opened up the first book, *Little Women*. She flipped through the pages, catching short phrases as they flew by. Almost instantly, the whole story came back to her. It certainly was romantic. Now, how did the guy and girl get started? Finally, Torie found the right scene.

But it was definitely wrong for her, she realized. They met in a snowball fight. Unfortunately, it was May in the real world right now. The only thing that Torie could throw at Kyle this time of year would be clumps of dirt and rocks. And Torie didn't consider that romantic at all.

Then she tried another of her favorite books, *Wuthering Heights*. But this one was no help, either. First of all, the guy in the book was a lot different from Kyle. He was a gypsy beggar. Also, the guy and the girl grew up together in the same house. It was definitely too late for Torie's family to try to adopt Kyle.

After going through a few more books, Torie started to laugh at how silly some of the ideas were. They worked fine in books, but Torie could hardly act them out herself. When she spotted *Jane Eyre* she took it down from the shelf; it was one of her favorite classics. As she idly flipped through the book, she found herself smiling at the scene where the hero and heroine first meet.

In this scene, the man, Mr. Rochester, was riding down the road on his horse, while the girl, Jane Eyre, was walking along the same road. It was a bitter, cold night. Suddenly, the man's horse slipped on some ice and both man and horse went down. Mr. Rochester had sprained his foot and was in pain, so Jane went forward to help the stranger. . . .

What if the reverse happened, and Kyle had to help me? Torie thought. *It would be the perfect way to meet without him knowing it!* Torie smiled to herself. *Not a bad idea. Not a bad idea at all.* She tucked all the books back in their proper place on the shelves and leaned back into a stretch. Then, during a nice, long hot bath, Torie worked out all the details of their "accidental" meeting.

*　　*　　*

The next day was Friday. With a month of school left before vacation, Torie could feel Summer Fever in the air already. Everybody in school was mentally out for the weekend as soon as the first-period bell rang. As for Torie, she had her mind on what she would do at exactly three-sixteen that afternoon, and she was more than a little nervous about it.

When she met Jo and Wendy at lunch, Torie didn't mention her plan. She was sure neither Wendy nor Jo would ever have approached a boy with an idea straight out of *Jane Eyre*.

As she sat down next to them in the cafeteria, Jo said, "How you doing, Tor? Anything *new*?"

"Not yet," Torie answered, shrugging her shoulders.

She knew Jo was referring to Kyle, but Jo had the good sense not to press the point, and Torie was relieved to be able to just say no and not go into the subject at length.

"So, do you two want to come to Mitch's practice with me this afternoon?" said Jo as she was eating a salad. "I guess we'll go to Romagnoli's for pizza or someplace after."

"Maybe," answered Wendy, munching on a sandwich. "I'm supposed to be studying for a math test, but that's not too appealing."

"I'd vote for soccer, too," said Jo. "How about you, Tor?"

"No—I'm going to go—straight home," said Torie, fiddling with the strap of her purse. She hadn't even gone to the lunch line for anything to eat. Her appetite seemed to have disappeared.

"Why are you going home?" asked Jo. "Your folks have something planned?"

"No," said Torie absently, "they're not even going to be there. My mom and dad are meeting each other after work, and they're going out with her boss or somebody." That much was the truth.

"So come with us," said Jo.

"*No*," said Torie with more emphasis than she'd meant.

"All right, all right," said Jo. "Chill out."

"Sorry," said Torie.

After that she really did try to keep her cool, but she got more and more nervous as the day drew on and came closer to the time for "Operation Meet Kyle."

By the end of the school day, Torie wasn't sure she could go through with it at all. Somehow, though, she managed to get up the nerve to give it a try.

After school Torie spotted Kyle's old gray Jeep parked by the sidewalk that surrounded

28

the parking lot, and she felt a surge of hope. Still, if Kyle had driven away before she got there, a part of Torie would have been very relieved.

There must have been a hundred students running toward the parking lot, hooting and hollering, mock-fighting each other, laughing, kissing. It sure was Summer Fever time. Cars fired up and spun out one by one as Torie reached the parking lot.

Walking along the sidewalk, Torie tried to look as if she weren't trying to look any particular way. She pretended to be simply waiting for a ride. Actually, she was mentally rehearsing the scheme she had borrowed from *Jane Eyre* to lure Kyle Fontana into her life.

As she imagined it, she'd casually stroll past the driveway out of the parking lot just as Kyle was pulling out. Her books would fall. He'd hit the brakes. He'd hop out of his car. He'd go to Torie's side. . . .

But *when* was it going to happen? Torie kept up her charade, walking back and forth for almost half an hour, until she started to feel like a total fool.

Pretty soon, there were only a few cars left in the parking lot, with no sign of Kyle anywhere. Meanwhile, two other guys had offered Torie rides home, and she had turned them both down.

Torie was growing more and more furious. She was mad at herself for resorting to such a phony, complicated way to get up the courage to talk to Kyle. And she was mad at Kyle for no reason. Just because she felt like it.

To make matters worse, Torie had missed the after-school bus, and she couldn't even call her parents for a ride. They weren't going to be home until late that evening.

Chapter Four

Tired and cranky, Torie stopped walking to empty a stone out of her right shoe. She had taken the back roads home from school instead of the highway, so none of her friends would see her. Unfortunately, the back roads were pretty rocky and steep. They made a long walk home seem even longer.

In one sense, though, taking the round-about route had paid off. At least Torie didn't have to face anyone she knew. Her hair was matted flat against her head from all the sun and sweat, and her shoes and stockings were caked with dust. Torie felt like a total wreck. All she wanted was to get home, shower, fall into bed, and forget the world. Thankfully, her house was just around the corner on the main road up ahead.

As Torie finally turned left at the corner of her street, her eyes widened in disbelief.

Kyle was driving down the road toward Torie's house, just as she was walking up to the house from the other direction.

Something inside her told Torie to duck before Kyle had a chance to see her looking like such a mess. She still had time to try to sneak along the side of the house and go in through the back door. He would never even see her. But her brain must have been as tired as her legs. Torie just kept walking along the sidewalk up to the house.

Kyle's Jeep screeched to a stop directly in front of her house, and he jumped out over the side without opening his door. He leaned against the side of the Jeep and watched her as she walked toward him.

Before she could even think of a proper response, Torie blurted out, "What are you doing here?"

"Fine, thanks," said Kyle sarcastically. "And how are you?"

"Oh—I'm sorry. I—didn't expect to see you here," said Torie. She tried fluffing up her hair with her fingertips, but she didn't want Kyle to notice what she was doing. Putting on as nice a smile as she could, under the circumstances, she said, "I'm just surprised to see you."

Kyle sat on the hood of his Jeep and drummed his fingers against its surface. "I'm barging in, I know," he said apologetically. "But I have a reason. Do you realize what you did to me?"

Torie couldn't imagine.

"You took my bottle of soda," he went on in mock anger. He let just enough of a smile break through to let Torie know he was kidding her. "I wasn't even finished drinking it!"

Torie had to force herself not to burst out laughing. With one joke and that super cool way of his, Kyle had made her feel terrific in one minute flat.

"Oh, yeah?" she said, playing along with him. "For your information, the soda you gave me was warm, not to mention the fact that there wasn't even a straw!"

Kyle started to laugh, but Torie kept it up a little longer. "Of course, it was better than the hamburger you forgot to bring me."

"I'll take care of that right now," said Kyle, standing up straight a few inches from Torie.

"Oh, really?"

"Sure—let's go," said Kyle.

"Where?"

"I'll buy you a burger. The best one in town."

Torie thought about it, for about one second. "Okay," she said, "but I'd just like to get changed. Could you wait a few minutes?"

"Actually, I have to make a couple of phone calls," said Kyle.

"Well, my folks aren't home—" said Torie.

She hadn't even finished before Kyle was hopping back into his Jeep. "Okay. I won't come in. I understand," he said. "I'll go use the pay phone at the Seven-Eleven. Be back in half an hour. Bye."

"Bye," said Torie. Kyle was already rolling down the road. "Can't he ever stay in one place for one minute?" she said aloud as she watched him drive off.

Hustling into the house, Torie ran up the stairs where she quickly undressed, got into the shower, and turned up the water full blast.

The shower helped clear her head, which had been spinning ever since she saw Kyle at her house. Torie was absolutely giddy about finally going out with Kyle.

What was it about Kyle? Maybe it was the way he always seemed to do whatever he wanted without a second thought. *Unlike me,* Torie thought. She rarely did anything that she hadn't carefully considered or planned. *And look at what all my planning got me,* she thought. *If I hadn't tried that silly charade in the parking lot, I wouldn't have gotten so filthy and sweaty and sore.*

Only one thing still worried her about Kyle: What if he turned out to be *too* different from her? What if they had absolutely nothing in common? Worse, what if Kyle was *too* strong, too fast for her to handle?

Today may tell, Torie told herself. *Today may tell.*

Dressing quickly but carefully, Torie slipped on her black jeans skirt and a blousy, pale yellow cotton top—cute but very casual. She tugged on her black flats. She looked herself over in the mirror and, last thing, dabbed on just a touch of blush and a little lip gloss.

By the time Torie had gone back outside, Kyle was back. He was waiting for her in the front seat, fidgeting with the radio. Although the sky was still a deep blue, a few fluffy clouds on the horizon were already tinted pink as the sun began to sink lower.

"You look great," said Kyle, hopping out again to open the door for Torie.

"Thanks," said Torie. She *felt* great, although she was pretty nervous.

Kyle pulled away, and they headed out of Torie's neighborhood. For a moment, the two of them simply sat in awkward silence—at least it was awkward for Torie. She had a million questions on her mind.

Trying to start somewhere, anywhere, Torie said, "Where do you live?"

"RD four," answered Kyle.

"Oh—outside of town?" said Torie, turning her head to Kyle. With the lengthening shadows of late afternoon, his strong, tanned profile had taken on mysterious planes.

"My family has a few hundred acres a little west of here," said Kyle.

"A few hundred acres! What is it, a farm?"

"A horse farm," he said. "The Fontana Breeders."

"Oh, I've read about them," Torie said, remembering an article in the local paper. "You raise horses that run and jump and stuff. Didn't you have a horse that was in a really big competition last year?"

"Well, we breed about a hundred horses a year, and most of them end up someplace. But, yeah, we did have one finalist in the nationals last year."

"Wow! Did your father have much to do with it?"

"Uh, not really," said Kyle, stopping the Jeep. "That one was pretty much all mine."

Kyle had pulled up to the Royal Diner, a big, shiny place with aluminum walls, a counter with swivel stools, and rows of booths covered with bright red vinyl. It had been in Arlenton since the 1950s. But, with the newer fast-food places all around it on the highway, Torie had never been in the diner before.

"Is this okay with you?" Kyle asked.

"Sure," said Torie a little hesitantly.

They got out of the Jeep, and as they entered the diner, Kyle very gently held her by the waist to lead her to a booth. When he touched her that way, it came as a complete shock to Torie. She wasn't used to a boy who was so comfortable with a girl on the first date.

Glancing around, Torie didn't see anyone from school or even anyone who looked familiar at all. Most of the customers looked as if they were from out of town.

Once they were both settled in the booth, Torie said, "You know, you were really a big surprise when I came home from school. How did you know who I was, and where I lived?"

"I heard your name in detention hall last week," Kyle explained as he opened a menu. "I don't know if you noticed me there."

"Oh, yeah," said Torie, looking down at her menu. "I think I did see you."

"Also, we're in the same class. We're both juniors," said Kyle.

"Really?" said Torie, looking up at Kyle again. He was fooling around with his napkin before he laid it flat on his lap.

"You have to try the burgers here. They're great. They're really thick and juicy, not like at the other places around here," said Kyle. "Anyway, I guess we're in all different courses. I'm not in College Prep.

"Besides, I don't hang around the school much," he continued. "I'm not real big on sports and school events and all. Can't stand crowds. Like, I would have been at your house sooner today, but I don't want anything to do with the mob scene in the parking lot on Fridays. I'd rather make some phone calls or something for half an hour. You know what I mean?"

"Well, sure," Torie said, while she put the pieces together in her mind. At least now she knew why he was late and she had to do all that walking. "What kind of phone calls do you have to make all the time?"

"Business," said Kyle. "Horse matters. Sales. Maintenance. You know."

"No, I don't know, really," said Torie. "I never learned much about horses in any of my classes. What classes do you take? What are you into?"

"Oh, boy—I take a lot of classes, but I'm

not really 'into' any of them," said Kyle. "I'm lousy with books. Besides, I know exactly what I'll be doing after school—working the horses with my folks."

When she heard that, Torie started thinking that she and Kyle might indeed turn out to be very different types of people. "Well," she said, "I've read about plenty of successful people who aren't exactly straight-A types in school. You know, Hemingway never went to college."

"Is that right?" said Kyle. "Who's he?"

Torie put her menu down. At first, she assumed the remark was one of Kyle's wisecracks. But by the completely serious expression on his face, Torie could tell he wasn't kidding. "Ernest Hemingway," she answered. "The writer."

"Like you," said Kyle, smiling.

"Me? Like Hemingway? I wish," said Torie, as the waitress headed toward the booth.

Before she reached them, Kyle asked Torie, "Know what you want?"

"Sure," she said as the waitress approached their table. "I guess I'll try that famous hamburger, with fries."

Kyle ordered for them both, and to Torie's surprise she didn't mind his ordering for her at all. After the waitress left, Torie continued,

"Now, I thought you were going to tell me how you found my house."

"I checked the phone book for your number and address, and after I got it I knew right where to go. I know your street, from a distance. I can see the tops of the houses from the farm."

"The tops of the houses?" Torie repeated, but what she was thinking about was her bedroom window. The grazing fields and farmhouse she always loved to look at from her room—they must be Kyle's!

When the waitress came back with their orders, Torie had one more question she had to ask Kyle. She took a bite of her burger to stall for time and build up her nerve. Finally she got it out.

"I hope you know that this whole thing is a little weird," Torie said. "I mean, we don't even know each other. You didn't even ask me out, really. You just showed up at my door. And here we are. I don't understand it. I mean, *why*?" She sat back in her seat. "Really—*why*?"

"You seem different," said Kyle. "So—I wanted to."

"That's all? You 'wanted to'?" said Torie. "You mean, you're in the habit of just picking yourself up and doing whatever you want?"

"I guess I am," said Kyle calmly.

"And what if I didn't want to go out with you?" said Torie, wondering how anyone could act so sure of himself.

"I guess we wouldn't be here now," said Kyle with a smile, and Torie smiled back.

They both finished their meals quickly. "Kyle—I'd better get going," Torie explained. "My folks aren't home, and they didn't know I would be going out."

"I see," said Kyle quietly. He asked for the check, paid for dinner, and took Torie's hand to help her up from the booth.

In the Jeep on the way to Torie's house, neither Torie nor Kyle said very much. Torie was trying to absorb what just went on. She didn't have the faintest idea what *he* was thinking.

By the time they reached Torie's house, it was getting dark out. It was that time of night when you could already see the moon, even though the sky was still dark blue. Torie could tell that her parents weren't home yet because the front-porch light wasn't on.

Kyle walked Torie up to her front door. As the two of them stood on the porch, Torie didn't know what to expect. She imagined Kyle capable of anything—anything he wanted.

"Torie," he said, holding her firmly by the shoulders. "I'll see you again real soon. Okay?"

Torie lowered her head and didn't answer. She didn't know how, right then and there.

"Okay?" he asked again. "Tomorrow night."

Torie lifted her head up in surprise.

"If you don't want to," Kyle told her, "just say so." He inched his body slightly closer to hers. He cupped her face in the palms of his hands. And he kissed her on the forehead, so softly, as he whispered to her, " 'Night, now."

Chapter Five

"Hey, Jo!" Torie's voice was an odd combination of a whisper and a shout as she walked through the back door of Jo's house early Saturday morning. The two of them had started walking right into each other's houses, without knocking, back when they had been third graders together.

Torie hustled straight through the kitchen and into the main hallway of the long, low, ranch-style house Jo's parents had built the year Jo was born. "Jo!" she called, heading toward her best friend's room.

"Yo!" said Jo from behind Torie, popping out of the bathroom. Her robe was getting all wet as she towel-dried her hair. "Hi, Tor. You should have come by a little earlier. You could have come right in the shower with me."

"Excuse *me*, Sleeping Beauty," responded Torie, trying to be just as sarcastic as Jo. Now that it had sunk in, though, Torie did feel somewhat silly about barging in as she did. But she just *had* to tell Jo about what happened to her last night.

"Come on in my room," said Jo. "What's up?" She pulled open her closet and started sifting through her outfits to find something to wear. Torie flopped down on the bed.

"You're not going to believe it. It's too weird," said Torie.

"What?" said Jo. She pulled out a pair of jeans and a yellow button-down shirt, slipped them on, and checked out the outfit in the mirror above her dresser.

"Yeah, what?" said a voice in the doorway behind them. Torie and Jo turned around, surprised.

"Wen!" said Jo. "You're here, too? What going on?"

"That's what I want to know!" said Wendy. She walked over to Torie and sat down on the bed next to her. "I was just sitting in my house minding my own business, and I saw Torie run in here. I figured *something's* happening. So—let's have it. Spill. Shoot."

44

"Don't ask me," said Jo. "This one's Torie's."

"Oh, yeah?" said Wendy, lying down on Jo's bed next to Torie. "Well, I'm ready."

"It's not *that* big a deal," said Torie. "I just had this date—"

"Who with?" asked Jo, with her back to Torie and Wendy. She still had the yellow shirt on, but she started looking at some other tops, anyway.

"Kyle Fontana."

Jo turned around, surprised.

"Who's that?" Wendy asked them both.

"Mr. Mystery," said Jo. "So, you did it!" she told Torie. "You finally took my advice! What did you say to him?"

"Nothing," said Torie. "Actually, I didn't even talk him into it. He just showed up at my house."

"Of course," Wendy chimed in, "I understand. Mr. Mystery just showed up, in his Mystery Mobile—"

"In a Jeep, actually," said Torie.

"Excuse me," said Wendy, "In his Mystery Jeep—"

"Cool it, Wen!" scolded Jo, buttoning up her shirt. "Now, Tor, what do you mean, 'He just showed up'?"

"I'm not really sure what happened myself. I mean, this guy's so—different."

"He sounds weird," said Jo.

"*He's* not weird," Torie snapped back. "He just does weird things."

"That makes perfect sense," cracked Wendy, sitting up.

Ignoring Wendy, Jo asked Torie, "Like what? Weird things like what?" She sat down on her bed in front of Torie and Wendy.

"Like, school doesn't seem to matter to him. He does whatever he wants," said Torie. "That's what's incredible—to me, at least. I never met anybody like him."

"Who in the world are you two talking about?" asked Wendy.

"That guy we saw in the Jeep outside school that afternoon," said Torie. "You know who he is? You know the big horse breeders who run the farm out in the country? That's Kyle. That's his family—the Fontana Breeders."

"Whoa!" said Wendy. "I've read about them. They own something like a dozen horses. They're *loaded*."

"Oh, really?" said Torie. She hadn't even thought about that aspect of Kyle's family business.

Jo got up and went over to her dresser, where she kept her makeup. "Where'd he take you?" she asked as she began to apply blush.

"Well," said Torie, "are you ready?" She

glanced at them dramatically. "He took me to—the Royal Diner."

"Naturally," said Wendy. "Only the *best* for the Fontana Breeders."

"Actually, the place is neat," said Torie with a giggle. She fell back on the bed and looked up at Jo's ceiling. "You know, I think I really like this guy. But I'm not sure I know why. We don't seem to have anything in common. I don't think he can even read."

Jo stopped in the middle of doing her makeup. She turned around and stared at Torie as she spoke.

"I'm only kidding. But he's not into books like I am. Can you believe it, he didn't know who Hemingway was! Anyway, I don't know *what* to think right now," Torie went on. "He hasn't given me the *chance* to think anything. And I'm supposed to go out with him again, already—tonight!"

"When did he ask you—when you were with him last night?" said Jo.

"Actually, he didn't ask me at all," said Torie. "He sort of just told me we were going out tonight. That's one thing that scares me."

"Are you going to go?" asked Wendy.

"I don't know," said Torie. "It's too much, too fast for me. I don't know if I should."

"I have an idea, Tor," said Wendy.

"No thanks, Wen, whatever it is," said Torie. "I don't need you taking this particular date off my hands."

"That wasn't my idea," said Wendy, standing up. "And it just so happens that I couldn't do that tonight, anyway. I'm going to a party. Kazuko Sato is having an incredible bash."

"So what's your idea?" said Torie. All she really knew about Kazuko was that she was one of the most popular girls at Arlenton.

"Never mind her idea," said Jo. "I know what you should do. Here's the solution to your problem. Go out with Mr. Mystery tonight, if you want to. But you make sure to tell him exactly where you want to go. Tell him you want to go to Kazuko's party, and don't take no for an answer.

"The thing is, Wendy and I will go, too," Jo continued. "Mitch will drive us over. That way, we can keep our eyes on you two. It's going to be hard for Kyle to go too fast with half of Arlenton High there. Besides, if he makes you uncomfortable, we'll be right there to the rescue!"

The way Jo described it, the plan sounded reasonable enough to Torie. She wasn't convinced that it was necessary. But it didn't sound as if it could hurt, either.

Jo sat down on her bed right next to Torie.

"That is," she said, looking straight into Torie's eyes, "*if* you want to go out with him. What do you want to do, Tor?"

"Well . . ." said Torie, starting to smile.

"You want to," said Jo. "You want to go bad, girl. I can tell."

Chapter Six

Sitting cross-legged on her bed, Torie stared at the notebook on her lap. She had gotten home from Jo's house two hours before, and she'd been working on her story ever since. But no one would ever guess it from looking at the blank pages of her notebook.

How could she write? The telephone was constantly ringing—or did she merely *notice* it more than usual?

Worse yet, only two of the calls were for Torie. One was from Jo, to see if Kyle had called yet. And the other was from Wendy, also to see if Kyle had called yet.

Torie looked down at the page again. All she had written were two short sentences:

I want to go to a party. I will meet you there.

* * *

Unfortunately, this had nothing whatsoever to do with the plot of her story.

Finally Torie got a third call. "For you, Tor!" Torie's mom called from downstairs. She picked up the phone on her desk and held her hand over the receiver for a few seconds, preparing her best cool-and-casual voice.

"Hello," said Torie.

"Hi, Tor," said Jo. "Any word from Mr. Mystery?"

"No!" said Torie. "And will you please stop calling me constantly about it?"

"I only called you once, an hour ago," said Jo.

"Oh, right," said Torie, calming down. "Sorry."

"Since he hasn't called you, I'm going to call Mitch now and find out what time he's going to pick me up. I'll call you right back. Sit tight. All right?"

"All right," Torie agreed. "Bye."

"Bye."

The phone rang right back, and Torie snapped it up to find out what time to be ready. "What's the plan?" Torie said.

"Hi," said Kyle. "I don't think I have the right number. Is Victoria Hilliard there?"

After the way she answered the phone, Torie

would have hung up had she thought quickly and clearly enough. Instead, she mumbled, "Hi. It's me. Hello."

"Oh—I'm calling about tonight," said Kyle. "I'll pick you up at eight o'clock."

Kyle's take-charge manner threw Torie off guard. Then she noticed her note pad. Thank goodness for the written word, she thought, reading straight off the paper: "I want to go to a party. I will meet you there."

"Well, I don't really like parties very much, Tor," said Kyle. Whether or not he noticed it, he didn't mention the strange, stiff way Torie told him what to do. "But, okay," Kyle agreed reluctantly. "What's the time and place?"

Torie yanked the phone book from under her desk and looked up Kazuko's address. "Thirteen West Judith Drive," she read aloud. "Um—eight o'clock?"

"Okay, Torie—if that's what you really want," said Kyle. "See you there."

"Bye," Torie hung up and plopped right down on her bed with the phone still in her right hand. She wasn't sure if she had done the right thing.

Lying flat on her back, Torie dialed Jo. As she spoke to her, she was looking out her bedroom window at a dimly lit farmhouse outside of town.

"Hey, I've been trying to reach you, but the line's been busy," said Jo. "I just talked to Mitch. We'll pick you up at seven o'clock."

"Make it seven-thirty," said Torie. "I don't have to be there till eight."

"Oh, you finally made arrangements with Kyle," said Jo. "Well, we'll come at seven, anyway, and hang out at your place."

"Seven-thirty," said Torie firmly. "Bye."

Torie wanted to take her time to get dressed that night. First she took a long, deep, steamy bath, then a cool shower. She even had enough time left to put her hair up in a clip, with just a touch of gel.

She wore a navy blue T-shirt dress that stopped a couple of inches above her knees. A pair of low heels dressed up the outfit slightly, in a funky, thrown-together way. Then, her makeup: a little blush. Some gloss—no, for a party at Kazuko Sato's, Torie put on lipstick and even a hint of black eyeliner.

While she was waiting for Wendy and Jo to pick her up, something worried Torie. Kyle hadn't sounded too enthusiastic when she told him she wanted to go to the party. Kyle was definitely unpredictable, and right now, Torie didn't know him well enough to be sure how he would act at Kazuko's party.

What if Kyle got a little too "wild"? What if

he didn't mix well with Kazuko's group of Arlenton hotshots? What if he embarrassed himself—and Torie—with something dumb like his comment about Hemingway? What if he didn't say anything all night? What if he even punched out somebody? Torie would *croak.*

Naturally, she didn't say a word about her fears on the way over to the party. Had she wanted to, she wouldn't have had a chance, anyway. Mitch and Wendy's date, Jeff, had so much to say about why they should have won the soccer scrimmage the day before.

When they pulled up in front of Kazuko's house, Jo gave Torie a nudge. There was Kyle's Jeep, already parked directly in front of the huge Tudor house where the Satos lived. *He's here,* Torie thought. *Well, at least they didn't kick him out!*

Mitch parked, the girls straightened out their outfits, and the guys immediately wrinkled them up again by holding the girls around their waists on their way into Kazuko's house. Torie trailed them, wondering why she had agreed to this.

Inside, Kazuko's house looked like the set of a music video. There was dancing and great, loud music and soda and food everywhere. The whole school seemed to be there, jamming every room of the enormous house.

Kazuko, wearing a white sundress that set off her gleaming black hair, caught up with Torie in the living room. "I'm glad you came," she said, almost shouting over the music. "Richie's in the den playing DJ; the entire soccer team is raiding the kitchen, and everyone who actually wants to talk is either outside or in the library."

"Have you seen Kyle Fontana?" Torie asked.

"I can't even find Michael," Kazuko replied. "And he's my boyfriend." She shrugged comically. "Just keep looking. He's bound to turn up."

Torie began her tour of the house as she searched for Kyle. She still had at least a dozen rooms left when she realized why she couldn't find Kyle. She should have been looking *outside* the house, from the start.

When Torie finally went out onto the back lawn of Kazuko's property, she hardly noticed Kyle at first. He was off by himself at the far end of the lawn, playing with a big, beautifully groomed Irish setter.

As soon as he saw Torie, he came toward her. The dog followed along, too, and to get rid of her, Kyle had to find a stick and throw it. While the dog was chasing it, Kyle took Torie by the hand and hurried into the house with her.

"We'd better get in there before she comes back, or I'll never be able to shake her," said Kyle.

"I can't believe you," said Torie, giggling. "There are hundreds of people here, and you hang out with the dog."

"I didn't know you'd be so jealous," said Kyle. "Of course, she *is* pretty beautiful."

"At least you've got good taste," said Torie teasingly. "Now come on. I want to find my friends."

"What about me?" asked Kyle as they plowed through the crowd in Kazuko's house.

"You want to see *your* friends?" asked Torie. "Well, sure. Where are they?"

"Actually, I don't have any friends here," said Kyle as he opened the door into the living room.

Torie stopped halfway through the door. "Are you sure?" she said. "The whole school is here!"

"I know a lot of kids who are here," he explained. "It's just that I'm not really close to any of them, particularly. But that has nothing to do with what I said before. What I meant was that I'd like to be with you."

"Oh—" Torie suddenly bumped smack into Jo, who was dragging Mitch along on her arm. Wendy and Jeff were right behind them.

"Excuse me, Torie," said Jo. Then every-body stood still, waiting for Torie to say something.

"Well," she said, "does everybody know Kyle?"

Jeff jumped in immediately, trying to be Mr. Life of the Party. "Now we do! Hey—how you doing?" he said. "You go to Arlenton?"

"Kyle Fontana," responded Kyle, extending his hand to shake with both Jeff and Mitch. "Aren't you Jeff Menell?"

"Last time I looked," answered Jeff, laughing loudly.

"We're in the same gym class," said Kyle.

"Oh, yeah?" said Jeff. "You know, I don't usually go to the regular gym classes," he continued. "Since I'm on the varsity team—"

"Hi," interrupted Mitch. "I'm Mitch."

"And this is Joanne," said Torie.

"Everyone calls me Jo," said Jo.

"Hi, Jo," said Kyle.

"And Wendy," Torie continued.

Kyle smiled and simply put his hands behind his back.

"So," Jeff said, taking Wendy's hand. "Let's dance."

Torie watched as Jo and Mitch followed. She was left standing alone with Kyle.

"Come on," she said, pulling him by the hand. But Kyle didn't budge.

"No, Tor," he said. "Sorry."

"Don't be silly," prodded Torie. "Let's go!"

"No!" he insisted, firmly. In fact, Kyle wouldn't dance with Torie once all night. He started out the evening very quiet, and as the hours passed, Kyle just became quieter. He scarcely spoke a word if he didn't absolutely have to.

Meanwhile, most of the other boys at the party seemed to be in a contest, each trying to outdo the next as the life of Kazuko's party. With all this going on, Torie was practically embarrassed by her sweet, big lump of a date.

By eleven o'clock Torie had had enough. She was ready to go home. She and Kyle went in search of Jo and Mitch to see when they were planning to leave. Mitch was holding court in the den, telling a joke Torie had heard before. It went on *forever*. Ten minutes later, after he finally got to the punch line, Torie whispered to Kyle, "Gees—doesn't he know when to stop?"

"I guess not," Kyle whispered back. "But give him a break, Tor. That's him. He's just doing what he knows how."

Kyle slipped his arms around Torie's waist, looking down into her eyes. "Now, let's dance," he said.

"Let's dance?" she said as he led her back to

the living room. "I've been trying to get you to dance all night! I thought you didn't know how."

"I never said that," said Kyle, with that cocky half smile of his. He drew Torie closer to him and slowly spun her out onto the dance floor. As she felt his arms cradling her, Torie let herself forget everything except how good it felt to be dancing with Kyle. Together, they swayed in time to a beautifully slow, hypnotic song.

"I've wanted to do this all night," said Kyle. "It just looks kind of funny when you're slow-dancing during rap music."

Torie giggled. "Kyle, will you tell me something?"

"What?"

"You've been so quiet all night. Is something wrong?"

He shrugged. "I tried to tell you on the phone—I'm just really not a party type of guy."

"Maybe you shouldn't have come," Torie said, feeling a bit guilty for having insisted on it.

"No way. Then I wouldn't have seen you tonight."

Torie smiled and wrapped her arms around Kyle's neck. *He really is different*, she thought. *He doesn't need to prove himself to anyone.* As she nestled her head under his chin, Torie could feel Kyle's heartbeat. She closed her eyes. She had never felt so safe.

"Hey, did you just fall asleep?" Kyle's voice was teasing her gently.

Torie looked up in surprise. The music had stopped, and she was still holding on to Kyle as if the dance had never ended. She felt herself blushing. "Be right back," she whispered before she got any redder.

She set off to find Jo and Wendy who were on the back lawn, talking with some girls from Jo's gymnastics team. Torie took Jo aside. "Listen, Jo," she said. "You can go home without me. I've got a ride."

"You riding home with Kyle?" Jo asked.

Torie nodded her head, smiling.

"Are you sure?" Jo looked at her with concern. "Because if you don't feel okay about him—"

"But I do feel okay about him." Torie couldn't hide the happiness in her voice. "I feel *extremely* okay about him."

Chapter Seven

"Whew," Torie said as she settled into Kyle's Jeep. "It's so quiet out here. I almost forgot what it sounded like *not* to have a stereo blasting."

Kyle sat for a moment before starting the motor. "You can even hear the crickets," he said. "They're early this year."

The night was warm and bright with stars, and with the top of the Jeep down, Torie felt as if summer had already begun.

As Kyle drove, Torie laid her head back on her seat and closed her eyes, loving the feel of the wind rushing over her face.

"Wake up," Kyle said, reaching over and gently tickling her on the ribs.

Torie laughed out loud and suddenly sat

upright. "Ooooh!" she said, putting her hands to her head.

Kyle hit the brakes. In a blink, he had pulled over to the side of the road.

"Torie—you okay?" he asked.

"Oh, sure, yeah," she answered. "I—just remembered something."

"What?" Kyle waited a moment, then headed back out onto the road.

"Oh, I just remembered that I didn't tell my parents about the party," said Torie. "I mean, I didn't tell them about *you*, that we were going to the party together."

"Ooooh," said Kyle, mimicking her. He spun the wheel to the right and stopped the Jeep at the curb.

Torie looked at him, puzzled. "Why'd you stop?"

"I didn't tell *my* parents about *you*, either," he said, teasingly.

Torie tried not to smile. "I just mean that I can't invite you in," she explained. "Actually, it's too late, anyway, now that I think about it. But I couldn't invite you in if I could. You know?"

"Clear as mud," Kyle assured her with a grin. He took both his hands off the wheel and turned to her.

"To tell you the truth," Torie went on a

little nervously, "you shouldn't even walk me to the door. If my parents saw it, it just wouldn't be worth the questions right now. Okay?"

"All right," said Kyle. He pulled back out onto the road and headed on to Torie's house. "So, I have an idea," he added.

Torie was almost afraid to ask. When she was in situations like this on other dates, she had seen plenty of "ideas" from guys who weren't nearly as impulsive as Kyle. As she looked over at Kyle, who seemed to be deep in thought, she was sorry she had brought the whole thing up.

Neither one of them said anything else until Kyle had pulled up directly in front of Torie's house. "Here's my idea," he said.

Torie slowly sneaked her hand onto the door handle, in case she needed to make an emergency exit.

"This is all you have to do," he said. "*Tell your parents about me, Torie.* If you think you ought to do something, you ought to do it!"

Torie let go of the handle.

"Would you do that?" Kyle asked. "So you can stop worrying so much?"

"Well, sure," Torie said, totally surprised.

"And one more thing," said Kyle. He turned

to her and took both her hands in his. "I want to kiss you, Torie. But not here and now if it's no good for you." Then Kyle gave her the slightest, softest, shortest kiss on the lips. "So, I owe you a *real* one," he said. "Don't forget."

"I won't," Torie whispered. "Good night."

"Night now, Torie."

That moment stayed with Torie through the night and was with her the next morning when she woke to sounds of the phone ringing. Still feeling as if she were in the middle of a lovely dream, Torie picked up the phone on her night table.

"Good morning," Kyle said.

"Mmmm?" Torie muttered into the phone.

"This is Kyle. I just called to tell you 'Good morning.' That's all."

"Oh, Kyle—I'm still asleep," Torie said. Slowly she pulled her pillow up behind her back and tried to sit straight up.

"Sorry if I woke you," he said. "I'll see you later. Bye."

"Okay—oh, wait!" Torie said, waking up quickly. "*When* later?" She wanted to make sure Kyle didn't appear unannounced at her house again.

"Well, I have work here to do all day today," he answered. "How about tomorrow night?"

"Monday? A school night?" asked Torie. "I don't know. It's just about exam time."

"Oh," said Kyle.

Torie peered across her room at the calendar on the bulletin board above her desk. She had something scribbled on this coming Wednesday, and it gave her an idea. "How about Wednesday?" she asked.

"Sure," said Kyle. "I'll come over right after school."

Torie squinted at her calendar from across the room. "Could you make it—seven-thirty? After dinner?"

"Sure," agreed Kyle. "All right. Now, you have a great day, Tor. Bye."

"Kyle," Torie said right before she hung up. "Good morning!"

Flopping flat back on her bed, Torie stared up at the ceiling. She certainly hadn't expected *that* phone call.

She did expect Jo to call as soon as she woke up, and Jo didn't disappoint her. The phone rang only minutes after Kyle's call.

"Listen, Tor," said Jo, "Wendy and I are going over to Mitch's later. Why don't you come, too? He's going to get some other guys and we can all find out everything that happened to everybody at Kazuko's."

"No thanks," said Torie, knowing she wasn't

ready to talk about the last night; it was so special that she wanted to keep it to herself for then. "I want to get some writing done today," she told her friend. "Honestly."

Torie convinced herself that she hadn't lied to Jo by sitting down and making a sincere effort to write. But the story she had shown Mr. Moyer wasn't going the way she planned, and after crumpling up at least five sheets of paper Torie gave up and decided she had better go outside and take a break. She paced her yard until that bored her, and then took herself on a walk through the neighborhood, trying to figure out what was wrong. Why had the writing suddenly gotten so much harder?

I don't want *to write that story,* she suddenly realized, coming to a complete standstill in the middle of the sidewalk. Ever since Kyle had come into her life, the story had been taking a turn of its own. *About him,* she thought. *What I really want to do is write what's been happening with Kyle, and I've been fighting it, trying to stay on my original course.*

Torie headed back to her house, got a glass of juice, and settled down at her desk. With a smile, she began the story she wanted to write.

*   *   *

On Monday night Torie decided it was time to mention Kyle to her parents, since he was supposed to come over to her house on Wednesday. Still, she didn't want to make a big production out of it, so she tried to bring up the subject as calmly and casually as she could.

"I was just wondering," she began as she helped her mother load the dishwasher, "whether you have anything special planned for Wednesday night?"

"No, I don't think so," said Mrs. Hilliard. "Why? Is there something special you want to do?"

"Not really," said Torie, without lifting her eyes from the stack of dishes she was loading. "Maybe this guy's going to come over, if it's all right."

"I see," said Mrs. Hilliard, glancing at Torie out of the corner of her eye. "Anyone we know?"

"No. He's a guy in my class. He's just going to come over," said Torie, trying to get the explanation—and the whole conversation—over with. "Would it be okay?"

"Certainly," said her mother. Finally, they both stopped what they were doing and looked at each other. From the intense way her mother was watching her, Torie could tell she was trying to see just how important this boy was to her daughter. But Torie played it cool.

"Okay, I'll tell him it's okay," said Torie, turning to the sink to wash her hands, "If I feel like seeing him."

On Wednesday evening Kyle pulled up to Torie's house at seven-thirty sharp. Knowing Kyle, Torie was certain he had a precise idea of where he wanted to take her that night, whether it was out for dessert, a movie, or whatever. But she had something in mind, too.

"Hi," said Kyle, when Torie greeted him at the front door. "Let's go."

"Come in," said Torie, tugging him inside by the hand. She pulled him toward the back of the house, straight through the front room, where her mother was writing some checks and her father was going through a thick file of papers.

"Mom, Dad, this is Kyle," she said, wanting to get the introductions over with as soon as possible. "Kyle—my parents."

"Hi," said Kyle. He nodded toward her mother and shook hands with her dad.

"So, what do you kids have planned?" asked Mrs. Hilliard.

"A movie," Torie answered immediately, turning toward the rec room at the back of the house.

"What movie is that?" her father asked with mild curiosity.

"*Anna Karenina*," Torie answered. "It's on channel eleven at eight o'clock. I've been wanting to see it for a while now."

Kyle didn't budge, but he darted his eyes over at Torie, looking somewhat surprised.

Still sorting through his papers, Torie's father said, "That's always been one of my favorite books." He looked at Kyle and explained, "I convinced Torie to read it last summer. Have you read it yet?"

"What book is that, sir?" Kyle answered.

"Tolstoy," her father answered.

"Who?" asked Kyle.

"Who—has the time?" Torie interrupted. "With exams coming up and all. Come on, Kyle."

Mr. Hilliard gave Torie a look that said he knew exactly what she was doing, but before he could ask any more questions she led Kyle into the rec room.

Torie sat down on the couch. Kyle didn't; he stood in front of her, looking as if he was trying to be patient. "Okay, Torie," he said. "*Anna* what?"

"*Karenina*. It's Russian. Aren't you going to sit down?"

"Torie," he said as he sat down next to her, "you asked me to come over on this particular night—so we could watch a Russian movie?"

"It's not a Russian movie. It's an American movie. They made it in the nineteen thirties, I think. It's just based on a Russian book," she explained. "I think you're going to like it a whole lot."

"Why?"

"You'll see," Torie answered, flicking on the TV with the remote control.

Kyle fidgeted restlessly through the first half hour of the movie, and Torie began to worry. Maybe it hadn't been such a good idea, after all. She'd been sure that he would be as caught up in the dramatic saga as she was. Instead, he seemed torn between the instinct to be polite and sit through it and the urge to be honest and bolt.

Just as Torie was about to admit she made a mistake and suggest they go for a walk or something, Kyle sat upright, paying rapt attention to what was on the screen. "Hey, an equestrian competition," he said. "What beautiful horses—"

"I *thought* you would find this interesting," Torie said, adding silently, *only I had no idea this is what would interest you.*

"Look at the filly on the left," said Kyle, putting his arm around Torie and holding her close to his side.

Silent and still, they cuddled close through the rest of the movie. Torie's head was nestled against Kyle's broad, strong shoulder, and she could feel his heartbeat, steady and rhythmic and wonderfully reassuring.

The movie was almost over when Kyle gazed down and saw Torie's eyes were closed. "Pssst, Torie," he said. "Are you asleep? Can you hear me?"

She didn't respond at all.

"Good. I don't think I could say this if you were awake," he went on. "Torie, I never met another girl quite like you before. I wish I knew how to tell you the way you make me feel."

Chapter Eight

On Thursday after Spanish class Torie found Kyle waiting by her locker.

"What's up?" she asked.

He looked down at her and smiled, and a feeling of warmth washed over her. Just looking at him made her feel so good.

"Well," Kyle explained, "since you invited me over to your house to watch horses—"

"That's not why I invited you—"

"I thought it was only fair to invite you over to my place to see some real horses," he finished, ignoring her protest. "Can you come out to the farm on Saturday? We can have a picnic or something."

"I'll read you Russian novels," Torie threatened.

"Whatever you want," he said with that cocky grin. "I'll pick you up at ten." Then before Torie could say anything else, he was gone.

When the last bell of the day rang, Torie headed straight for Jo's locker. "You've got to help me," she told her friend. "An emergency shopping trip is called for."

Jo looked at her curiously. "What's the emergency?"

"I need to buy something 'country,' " Torie explained.

"As in work boots and overalls?"

"Not exactly," Torie said hesitantly.

"How about as in Nashville and country music?"

"I think that would be overdoing it. It's Kyle," Torie admitted shyly. "He's invited me for a picnic on his farm on Saturday, and I need something to wear."

Jo arched one eyebrow, a skill Torie had practiced in vain. "You never did tell me what happened after the party," she said thoughtfully. "But I guess this means you still like him."

Torie's voice was quiet as she answered, "Yeah, I still like him."

With Jo's help Torie tried on about fourteen outfits before deciding that she'd wear something she already had. But she did find a wide-brimmed straw hat that she loved, and though Jo thought it was "too country," Torie bought it anyway.

"So," Jo said as they left the mall, "what's the mysterious Kyle Fontana really like?"

"Well, I haven't exactly got him figured out," Torie confessed. "All I know is that I've never met anyone like him. He's real strong and gentle all at once. I always feel safe when I'm with him."

"He sounds really special," said Jo with a smile. "But Torie, he's so different—from everyone else, I mean. Wendy's been asking around about him and—"

"She's what?" Torie demanded indignantly.

"Relax, it's nothing bad. All she found out is that the only thing that seems to matter to Kyle Fontana is his horse farm. Make that two things: his horse farm and *you*."

That night Torie sat at her desk, her chemistry book spread open in front of her. Final exams were only weeks away, and it seemed that every night she had some year-end project or paper to do when what she really wanted to do was work on her story.

Ever since she had stopped trying to force her writing, Torie had felt positively inspired.

The story was flowing with a life of its own. It was definitely based on her and Kyle, although it seemed to move a lot more smoothly than real life. *For one thing,* she thought, staring down at her book, *it leaves out all the boring parts like chemistry class.*

The only problem, Torie realized with a sigh, *is that I barely have time to work on it.* She always saved her writing for the last part of the day, almost as if it were a reward for getting through the rest of her homework. But every night when her homework was done she'd curl up on her bed and write until she fell asleep. And over the past week, her project had gotten fairly involved and lengthy—very long for a story. She was already on page fifty-four, and there was still a lot more she wanted to add.

Torie hadn't shown the story to anyone, except the parts Mr. Moyer had made her show him after school, and she had never wanted to read it to him. Torie forced her attention back to the periodic table. *Tonight,* she promised herself, *I'll write about an invitation to a picnic.*

Torie woke up early on Saturday morning. The night before she and her mom had mixed up a jug of lemonade and made sandwiches and chocolate-chip cookies to bring to the farm.

By nine-thirty Torie was dressed in jeans and a soft blue sweater. That would be perfect for Kyle's place, she figured, since that was what he always seemed to wear. But she added a few important touches: a bandanna around her neck, some light makeup, and her new straw hat.

"Well, look at the little country girl," he said when he saw her.

"I'll take that as a compliment," said Torie, "coming from a country boy."

Kyle grinned and took Torie's bag for her. "Whoa, this is heavy! What do you have in here?"

"Just some things I cooked up," Torie answered with a wink.

Kyle drove through Arlenton then out onto the old rural roads. In ten short miles, everything changed so much. The houses gave way to open fields, and the air became more crisp and clear, smelling of new-mown grass. Even the sun seemed warmer, somehow.

"Here we are," said Kyle, pulling into the long drive that wound uphill to the farm.

"It looks different," Torie said.

"What do you mean?"

"Well," she answered, "from my bedroom

window it always looks like an old picture postcard with a tall white farmhouse, big red barn, and picket fences all around."

"And now?" Kyle asked as he parked beside the front gate.

"All these people," Torie said in amazement. "I never imagined it'd be so busy."

Workers were carrying sacks of feed into the barn, and a small man with a jockey's build was leading a gleaming black horse out of the stable. On the hill, Torie could see people taking photographs and measurements of a group of horses.

"Are you disappointed?" Kyle asked.

Torie shook her head, laughing. "Kyle, this place is *fantastic*."

Kyle draped their lunch bag over a shoulder, took Torie by the hand, and began the official guided tour of the Fontana farm.

"That's where we live," Kyle said, nodding toward the farmhouse. Torie could see the outline of a woman waving from one of the front windows. "That's my grandmother," he said as he returned the greeting. "We'll go up to the house a little later, but first I want to show you the farm." He led her down the dirt road that wound through the pastures.

"What are those people doing with the cameras and equipment?" Torie asked as they climbed the hill toward the first paddock.

"I'll show you," Kyle said, walking up behind a serious-looking man with a clipboard and a calculator. Working beside him, a woman laden with photographic equipment was taking pictures of a beautiful chestnut-colored horse.

"We have a major horse auction coming up in three weeks, and we need photographs taken of the horses we'll be entering," Kyle explained. "That's North Star, one of our best fillies."

Torie felt as if they were disturbing serious work. "We'd better leave them alone," she said.

"No, it's all right," Kyle said. "Besides, I want you to meet my parents." He waited until the photograph was taken, then said, "Mom, Dad—I'd like you to meet Torie."

"Oh—hi," said Torie. She took off her hat although she had no idea why. "Pleased to meet you."

"Well, hello there, Torie. I'm Dan Fontana." Kyle's dad tucked his clipboard and calculator under one arm and shook Torie's hand vigorously.

Mrs. Fontana snapped the lens cap onto her camera and smiled at Torie, looking for a moment very much like Kyle. "My name's Margaret, dear," she said. "Has Kyle shown you the colts yet? We've got four new ones in the stables."

"We're headed over to the west quadrant," said Kyle, "to have lunch. Maybe we'll look at the colts on the way back. There's just one thing, Dad. You'd better get Chuck hustling. He's burning two grand."

"Again?" Mr. Fontana frowned. "I'd better go talk to him. Thanks for letting me know."

As they walked back down the road Torie asked Kyle, "What did you just say to your dad?"

"Well, I saw that our stockman left a fresh shipment of feed out on the ground," explained Kyle. "It's vitamin enriched, and the additives lose potency in the heat—as much as five percent per hour in temperatures like we're supposed to get today. With five hundred cubic feet of the stuff, we could take a loss of—"

"Kyle," Torie interrupted, "you sound like my algebra teacher. I didn't realize you know so much about that kind of thing."

"Oh, yeah—I'm brilliant, when I'm talking about horse feed," said Kyle, kicking a rock out of the ground with the toe of his boot. "But not about Hemingway. Or Tolstoy."

"Oh," Torie said, sensing for the first time

that Kyle was uncomfortable about the things he didn't know. She didn't know how to respond to him, but she decided to give it some serious thought.

She looped her arm through his. "Now, if you think your horse food loses its strength in the sun, you should see what happens to me," she said. "Let's get going, while I can still walk!"

Arm in arm, Torie and Kyle climbed up the long ridge that rose behind the barns and silo. When they were just about at the top, Torie nudged Kyle in the side. "I bet you thought I couldn't do it," she said. "Wait, you want to hear something strange? This hill is the last thing I can see on the horizon when I look out my window. This is going to seem silly to you, but when I was a little girl, I used to think this very spot was the end of the world. I did. Every night I used to watch the sun set right here. Isn't that crazy?"

"No," said Kyle. He was watching her, smiling in a way that made Torie's head spin.

"I've got an idea," said Torie. "I'll race you the rest of the way up. Race you to the end of the world!" And before Kyle could answer she tore off, sprinting to the top of the ridge.

Kyle took off after her, but he didn't really

have a chance. Torie had the head start, and he was carrying the food.

"You little cheat," he called as he jogged toward her.

But Torie, standing on the crest of the ridge, barely heard him. "Oh, my gosh," she said softly. There, below her, were the main grazing grounds of the farm and the Fontana horses—more than a hundred of them, their sleek coats shining in the sun.

Kyle came up behind Torie and held her by the waist. "I was right," Torie said. "This *is* another world. Could we stay here for a while and watch the horses?"

"Sure, whatever you want." He held onto her a little more tightly, and Torie let herself slip softly back against him.

"How much of this land is yours?" asked Torie.

"Pretty much everything you see—all the open land, I mean," explained Kyle. "Actually, there's a lot more acreage out there than you'll usually find for the number of horses we have—an extra couple of acres per head.

"There aren't any fences there, either. Look. All the boundaries are natural—the stream, the woods on two sides, and this ridge," he continued, pointing out to the edges of the grazing grounds.

Torie found the farm fascinating. But what impressed her most was Kyle. When he spoke about the farm he seemed different, more peaceful, as if this was where he truly belonged.

"Just look at those horses, Torie," he went on. "Do you realize what wonderful creations they are? They're incredibly powerful, for one thing. Every one of them could kill a man. And it would, if you give it a good reason to do it. But, treat them right, and they'll lay down their lives for you. They just need to run free. You can't crowd them or cage them in. They have to have open air. It's in their blood."

"Kyle," said Torie, turning around to face him, "you sound as if you're talking about *yourself*. You do."

"Yeah," Kyle said, "they'd probably do about as well in school as I do."

"You're wrong," said Torie, pulling away from him.

Kyle grinned. "How many horses do you know who've read Hemingway?"

"I mean, you're all wrong about *yourself*," Torie explained. "Just because you haven't done too well in school doesn't mean you can't." She took a deep breath. "Maybe I've got no right to say this, but I think the only problem is that you don't care about school. And I can't figure out why. Can you tell me?"

"Oh, Torie," said Kyle, "I don't know. I guess, *this* is my life. It's all I've ever known. This farm, it's the only thing I've ever loved."

"Well," said Torie, taking his arm in hers, "at least now I know what I'm up against."

Kyle looked at her warily. "I don't know what you're planning," he said, "but I think I'm going to change the subject. Look down to the right, where the trees start to thicken," he said. "There's a stream down there. It's nice and shady. Come on."

They wound their way downhill, seeming to fly along the side of the ridge without any effort of their own.

Kyle took Torie's hand as they reached the stream and led her along the edge of the water to a small shady clearing. Wild grass blanketed the ground, and tall trees stood like walls protecting the cozy little spot.

"This is my very favorite place on the entire farm," said Kyle. "It's where I always come when I want to be alone."

Torie spun around in delight. "I can see why you love it," she said. "This is *wonderful*."

"Perfect for a picnic, that's for sure," said Kyle, pulling the lunch bag off his shoulder. "Let's see what you have in there."

"One thing at a time." Torie grabbed the bag from Kyle, sat down on the grass with her legs folded under her, and began emptying the bag. "Sandwiches—potato chips—cookies, homemade lemonade—and something else."

"What's that, Tor?" asked Kyle.

"For you," said Torie, handing him a thick manila envelope.

Kyle opened it quickly and pulled out a thick stack of paper. " 'By Victoria Hilliard,' " he read. "Torie, is this your story—what I heard the first time we met?" asked Kyle.

"Yeah."

"For *me*?" asked Kyle.

"For you to *read*, silly," she told him. "I made a copy of the whole thing for you."

Kyle flipped through the pages. "I didn't know you were this serious about your writing, Tor. This must have taken you a really long time to write. There are an awful lot of pages here."

"Precisely sixty-three pages, as of today," said Torie. "And it's not finished yet. I don't expect you to read the whole thing right here, you know. But you can take it with you. I'd like you to. I never showed the whole thing to anybody before."

"That's fair, Tor," said Kyle with a grin. "I never *read* anything this long before."

"Kyle," Torie said seriously, "you *could* read just the last chapter now, if you want to."

Kyle looked at her carefully. "All right," he said. Then he read the whole chapter, closely and carefully. Torie watched him nervously, wondering what he thought of her writing. At last he reached the final page, and Torie saw his eyes widen with surprise. He looked at her and smiled, then read the very last part aloud. " 'I never met another boy quite like you before. I wish I knew how to show you the way you make me feel.' "

"Actually, I didn't write that part," said Torie, blushing. "A very special person once said something like that."

"You weren't really asleep," he said softly. Then he took her in his arms and held her. Torie knew she'd never been so happy.

Chapter Nine

"Stay here for a while. I haven't seen you very much lately," said Torie.

"No, I really can't. I promised to help my mom put in the screen windows," said Jo. It had only been ten minutes since the girls had gotten off the school bus and Torie had just poured a couple of sodas and brought them out to her patio. And Jo was already getting up to go home.

"I can't hang around," Jo added dramatically, "*unless* you want to tell me everything about your big day at Kyle's. Then *I'll* tell *you* about my date with Mitch on Saturday."

"Honestly, Jo, I told you everything we did," Torie said. "We walked around, we had a picnic, Kyle read my story—"

Jo broke in laughing. "Do you mean to say

that this guy took you out in the middle of the woods, and the two of you were there on the grass, and he decided that this was a good time to catch up on his *reading*?"

Torie's mom cracked open the back door. "Girls, if you're discussing Kyle Fontana, you'd better lower your voices. He just came to the front door, and I told him he'd find you both around back."

"Oh, my gosh," said Torie. "I've got to get changed. Jo, you keep him busy for a while."

"Right," said Jo as Torie hurried inside.

A few seconds later Kyle rounded the corner of Torie's house. Jo wouldn't have recognized him. Nobody would have. Kyle's face was practically covered by a huge stack of books he was carrying in his arms.

"Over here," Jo told him. "Put them over here on the table."

Kyle placed the stack of books down. "Hi," was all he said.

"Torie's inside," Jo explained, staring at the books. "Funny—we were just discussing how much you like to read. I guess Torie wasn't kidding."

"Hi, Kyle," said Torie, coming back out in exactly the same outfit she had been wearing. Once she thought about it, she realized there was absolutely nothing wrong with it.

"Hi, Torie," said Kyle. "I'll be right back." And he disappeared around the side of the house as quickly as he had appeared.

"Cute outfit," Jo told Torie. "A big improvement."

"Hey, I thought you had to go home," said Torie with a grin. She sat down in front of the stack of books on the table. Tilting her head sideways, Torie looked over the titles. "What the—"

"Maybe he wants to go on a real long picnic," teased Jo.

"Jo"—Torie was trying not to smile—"don't you know what time it is? You'd better get out of here or your mother's going to kill you."

"No," said Jo, "I think you were right before. I should stay for a while."

Moments later Kyle returned with another stack of books. "This is it," he said, placing the books next to the first pile.

Torie couldn't figure this scene out at all, but she decided to play it cool. "Kyle, you must be tired from lugging all those books," she said. "Let me get you a soda, okay? And, Jo—while I'm inside, I'll give your mom a ring for you and tell her not to worry. I'll tell her you *left already*."

"All right, all right," Jo grumbled. "Don't

bother. I'm leaving now. So long. Have fun—reading."

It does look as though Kyle came over to read, Torie thought as she got the soda from the refrigerator. *But knowing Kyle, he's got something else planned.*

Kyle wasted no time filling her in. "I read your whole book," he announced.

"You mean, my story?"

"Torie, don't you realize what you've done? You've been working on that so hard for so long, it's not a story anymore. It's practically a book. It's really *long*."

"That's not enough," Torie said softly. "A book, a *real* book, is more than a big pile of pages."

"But I think what you wrote is terrific!"

Torie smiled at him, thinking that in Kyle she'd found a rare friend. "Thanks," she said, "I was hoping you'd like it. But, I don't want to hurt your feelings—"

"Hey, you don't have to worry about my feelings when it comes to this stuff," he said. "What are you going to say—that I don't know anything about literature? I know that. You know that. Your father even knows that now. But I know one thing that you don't know."

"What?" asked Torie.

"I know that when you want something,

when you love something, you should do something about it. And you shouldn't let anything in the world stop you."

"I still don't understand what you're getting at," said Torie.

"You should have your book published," Kyle said simply.

"*That's* the point of all this?" asked Torie, leaning back against her chair. "Are you serious? Kyle, I can't show my writing to anybody! I haven't even shown it to my oldest friend or my own parents, let alone perfect strangers. I *can't*."

"Yes, you can—at least you can try," said Kyle. "And I'm going to help you, Tor. Right now."

"Kyle, stop," said Torie. "I don't want to. Please."

Kyle went on as if he hadn't even heard her. "Listen, we're going to start by making a list of publishing companies. That's why I brought all these books here. The names and addresses of the companies are right inside the books, on the page next to the library card."

"Will you *stop*, please?" said Torie. "For goodness sakes, Kyle, I've seen a book before. I know that the names of the publishers are printed inside. But you didn't have to knock yourself out like you did just to get some names and addresses of publishing companies. You could have gotten the same information from a reference book. Didn't you ask the librarian what to do?"

"Well, no," said Kyle.

"Of course you didn't. Not big, pushy Kyle Fontana!" Torie said, suddenly angry. "Well, maybe it wouldn't hurt you to think a little more before you do things, instead of just marching ahead and doing whatever it is you feel like. And that especially means trying to tell me what I should do with my writing. And another thing—I know you mean well, but you really could *call* me before you just show up at my door!" Torie stopped herself before she went any further. She hadn't meant to blow up at Kyle like this, but it was beginning to seem as if he took a lot of things for granted.

There was a long, awkward silence. Finally, Kyle spoke. "You're right," he said softly. "I'm sorry, Torie." He reached over, took one of her hands and held it tightly in his. "Maybe I am too cocky. Maybe I should be a little more— like you."

"You're just fine, Kyle," Torie said, feeling a little remorseful. "But I'm not used to anyone coming on so strong with me. I've just never looked at things the way you do."

"Maybe we can both learn from each other," Kyle said.

"Maybe," Torie said, her anger rapidly fading.

"You think so?" Kyle suddenly had a mischievous glint in his eyes. "Good. Then we agree. Let's start working on getting your book published. Go get a pad and pencil. Then, you read me the name of each publishing company, and I'll write it down."

Torie simply stared Kyle straight in the eye for a moment. "Okay, okay!" she finally said. "Okay—if this means so much to you. It doesn't matter what we do anyway. No publisher could care about anything from a sixteen-year-old girl."

To Torie's surprise, the two of them worked very well together. When they had reached the next-to-last book on the pile, Torie said, "Well, it's working, Kyle. I *am* getting more like you. We're just about done, and I never even stopped to think about what we're doing. Now, could you tell me why in the world we're writing down information about so many publishers? Only one company can publish one book."

"I forgot, I guess," Kyle said a little sheepishly. "Then just pick one."

"*Which* one?" asked Torie. "I don't know one company from the next."

"Oh, then, let's try"—Kyle looked over the stacks of books till he found one particular book—"this one."

Torie read the cover. It was *Anna Karenina*.

"It's the only book here that I know has horses in it," Kyle explained, laughing.

Torie grinned wearily. "Fine with me. Okay—now what, Mr. Mastermind?"

"That's it," said Kyle. "I'll take care of everything. I have your book, I'll make a photocopy, put it in an envelope, and send it to the publisher with your return address."

"Well, okay," Torie agreed. "Let's just write up a letter to go along with everything. Could you hand me that note pad?"

Torie fiddled with the eraser on the tip of her pencil for a moment, thinking of what to write, and then started scratching ideas on the pad. Finally, she copied the letter neatly onto a clean sheet of paper. It read:

Dear Sir or Madam:

I am a sixteen-year-old girl and a junior at Arlenton High School. I have written the enclosed manuscript.

I do not know if my writing is very good. Also, I do not know very much about book publishing.

However, I realize that I will never find

out about either of these things unless I try. I have just learned this from someone very wise.

If you could read my manuscript, I would be very appreciative of any advice or criticism you may have.

Thank you very much.

Sincerely,

Victoria Hilliard.

Torie neatly ripped the letter out of her notepad, folded it, and handed it to Kyle just in time. Her mother was coming out onto the back steps. "Dinnertime, kids. We have a place set for you, Kyle. Would you like to stay?"

"Sure would," he said, "but can't. Thanks anyway." Kyle started loading the books in his arms. "'I haven't been home yet, and my own folks are expecting me for dinner. I have some chores to do, too. And nobody's going to believe me when I say I'm late because I stopped at the public library."

Chapter Ten

Torie's regular routine at school started to change. She and Kyle took different courses, often in different wings of the Arlenton High building, but they started to meet between classes whenever they could—usually once or twice a day. Torie looked forward to their time between classes as much as she used to look forward to the classes themselves.

The only time during the school day when Torie and Kyle could actually spend some time together was lunch period. Still, Torie wasn't ready to stop having lunch with Jo and Wendy every day. After all, Jo had never broken their routine so *she* could eat with Mitch and his friends from the soccer team. Then again, Torie had always wondered if Mitch had ever *invited* Jo to join him with all of his jock buddies.

On the day after Torie had written to the publisher, she and Kyle decided to meet outdoors as soon as they finished eating lunch. This way, Torie could see Jo and Wendy and still have some time with Kyle.

"What's my favorite author doing tonight?" Kyle asked as they walked along the edge of the soccer field toward the school. "Mind if I come over?"

"I can't," Torie said. "I mean I'd love to see you, but it *is* almost final exam time. Don't *you* have any work to do?"

"Are you kidding?" said Kyle. "It's only two weeks till the summer auction. You wouldn't believe how much work I've got to do."

"I meant *school*work," said Torie. "I know you never have any homework. Don't you have final exams, either?"

"What makes you think I never have any homework?" asked Kyle.

"Well, look at you. Stop right there. Don't move." Kyle stood still as Torie moved in front of him, face to face. "You're never carrying any books," she began. "Your hands are always in your pockets."

Kyle looked down at himself and shrugged. "Gee, you're right," he said. He took his hands out of his pockets and placed them around Torie's waist. "How's that?"

Torie tried not to smile. "Not now, please, Kyle."

He put his hands in his pockets again and leaned backward against the side of the school building. "I have homework," he explained. "I guess I just don't like to do it. It's the same with studying. I can't just sit there and read and think about—whatever—history, math. I have to *do* things. I'm not like you, you know."

Torie was a little afraid to ask her next question but decided to go ahead anyway. "Kyle, if you don't like to do your homework, what kind of grades do you get?"

"Well, they're not A's," said Kyle.

"I bet they're not B's, either—or even C's, half the time," said Torie. "And you're so smart. It's too bad that I'm the only person who knows it."

The bell rang to mark the beginning of the next period. "Come on," Torie said, "the least you could do is *show up* for class."

As they walked toward the door into school, Torie thought for a moment. "You know, it's not too late to make up for your bad grades," she said. "You could do it, if you studied really hard and did really great on your finals."

"Sure," responded Kyle halfheartedly. "A few A's would be great on my grade card. I could pin it onto my saddle, and show off in front of the fillies."

Torie let that wisecrack sink in for a moment, but she didn't respond. She and Kyle walked inside and started to separate to go to their classes. "Bye, Tor," said Kyle.

Torie turned around abruptly. "Kyle, wait!" she said. "I want to change my answer."

"What answer?"

"About coming over to my house tonight. It's fine if you want to. I'll meet you after school, at your locker. What number is it?"

"Six-oh-two," answered Kyle, looking somewhat confused by Torie's behavior. But before he had a chance to question her, Torie disappeared into the crowded hall of students.

When Kyle showed up at his locker after his last class, Torie was already standing there waiting for him. "You know, this is an honor," she said. "I haven't seen your locker yet."

"Not much to see," responded Kyle as he worked his combination and opened up his locker. It was almost empty, with nothing in it but a baseball cap and a few books that looked brand-new.

"Uh-oh!" said Torie. "It's a good thing you don't carry those books around. You never covered them! If a teacher ever saw you with

98

those books uncovered like that you'd get another detention pass."

Kyle gave her a cocky grin. "You know," he drawled, "you worry about the weirdest things."

"Never mind," said Torie. "Just bring them with us, and I'll cover them for you at my house. I'd feel better if I did. Okay?"

"All right," said Kyle. "But I don't think it's such a big deal." Reluctantly he took the books out of the locker and slung them under his arm. Torie had to suppress a smile as they walked out to the Jeep—she'd never seen anyone look so uncomfortable carrying books.

"Let's go out on the patio," Torie said when they got to her house.

Kyle set the books down on the wrought-iron table and straddled one of the lawn chairs. Immediately, he began drumming a complicated rhythm on the tabletop.

Torie stepped directly in front of him, took his books, and held them in her arms.

"Now it's your turn," she said, assuming a stiff, theatrical pose. "Kyle, I have come with a pile of books to teach you a lesson," she said dramatically.

"Oh, I get it." Kyle leaned forward against the back of the chair and folded his arms. "You're pretending to be me, when I came here yesterday."

99

"Now," Torie continued, "I'd like you to open each one of these books and read it."

"Okay, Tor. I'll go along with you," Kyle responded. He picked up one book and opened it to the first page. "Let's see who the publisher is."

"That's not what I meant," said Torie, sitting down in front of him at the table. "I want you to start reading the *whole book*."

"*What?*" Kyle slammed the book closed and glared at her. "What's going on, Torie?"

"Just what I said. Now it's your turn to listen to me, just as I listened to you yesterday about my writing."

Kyle took a deep breath, as if trying to summon patience he didn't have. Finally he said, "I really don't know what you're talking about."

"Yesterday you said you wanted to tell me something I didn't know," Torie began. "Now *I* want to tell *you* something *you* don't know." She knew she sounded as if she were lecturing him, but she couldn't help it.

"You're not as dumb as you think you are, Kyle Fontana. But you're not as smart as you think you are, either. You don't think you have to study. You think you're just a horse farmer who's never going to go to college. But I think I know you better than that. I think you really *want* to learn. You wish you knew more about things like—Hemingway and—"

"Tolstoy?" Kyle finished sarcastically. "Yeah. I've been dying to find out more about Tolstoy."

"Please," Torie said, "just hear me out. All I'm saying is that it's not too late. You've still got a chance to learn this semester's material and get decent grades. All you have to do is buckle down and study."

Kyle stared at her in disbelief. "What in the world has come over you, Torie?"

"You—you've come over me," she answered softly. "Remember what you said to me yesterday? You said a lot of things. You know, you can *really* talk when you get going. I couldn't shut you up!"

"Well, same to you."

"Thanks."

Torie and Kyle both smiled—almost laughed —at that point. But the whole conversation was much too intense to stop. And Torie still had a lot on her mind.

"You told me that when you really believe in something, when you really love something, you should do something about it," said Torie. "Well, I really believe in *you*, Kyle. You said that you shouldn't let anything in the world stop you. And I won't. I'm going to *make* you study, Kyle, just like yesterday you made me send my story to that publisher."

"Is that right?" said Kyle with a cocky, challenging grin. "And how are you going to do that?"

"Well, I have one idea," explained Torie. "Let's see. Finals are over in the first week in June, right? What's the date?"

"I don't know," he answered.

"Well, whatever the date is," Torie said, "we've got plenty of time." She gave Kyle a quick, light kiss. "And we can work together every day. Just you and me—and your books."

"My books?" said Kyle. "Gee, that sounds exciting."

Torie shrugged. "Of course, we don't *have* to see each other at all," she said, "if you don't want to."

Kyle gave her a look of sheer exasperation. "I want to," he said, "but I can't. I have to go home in the afternoons because of the big summer auction coming up. There's too much work to do during the day right now."

"All the better then," said Torie with a wicked smile. "You'll just have to come over to see me after dinner and study every *night*."

"Well . . ."

"Please, Kyle, just try it and see what happens."

He smiled ruefully and shook his head. "I can't believe I'm agreeing to this, but, okay."

"Do you promise?"

He raised his hands overhead in defeat. "I promise! You know something—you're even more stubborn than I am."

"Maybe," Torie admitted, satisfied that she had his word. "Now tell me, when is that auction?"

"It's always the first Sunday night in June," he answered. "Why? Ever been to a horse auction?"

"No."

"Then come with me."

"Did you say the first Sunday night in June?" she asked carefully.

"Sure did," said Kyle. "People and horses come in from all over the country. You've got to see it."

"Then, no—that's the beginning of finals week. I can't possibly go." Torie put an arm around Kyle's neck. "And Kyle," she whispered, "you can't go, either."

Chapter Eleven

Kyle was as good as his word. On Wednesday, the day after he agreed to begin studying, he showed up at Torie's house at seven o'clock sharp.

Torie began by taking out a calendar. "Let's see what we're up against," she said. "Today's Wednesday, May twenty-third. And finals begin June fourth. That gives us almost two weeks to do a whole year's worth of schoolwork."

"No problem," said Kyle sarcastically.

"Well, it won't be easy," Torie admitted with a sigh. "But nothing's impossible."

Kyle shot her a skeptical look but refrained from comment.

They settled in together on the floor, leaning back against the couch, with their books set up in front of them on the coffee table. Torie opened up her English text to chapter twelve, and she opened up Kyle's American history book to chapter one.

Everything went well—until about seven-oh-five.

"I could use a soda," said Kyle, getting up and heading into the kitchen. "Want one?"

"No—we just sat down!" said Torie. "Did you read anything yet?"

"Yeah," answered Kyle from the kitchen. "The Spanish monarchs sent Columbus in search of spices for their food." He hurried back in and sat down again—on the other side of Torie, away from his own books. "Spicy food always makes me thirsty," he added with a smirk, taking a swig from a can of cola.

"You're a nut, you know that?" said Torie, taking Kyle's history book and plopping it down in front of him.

"That's what they told Columbus!" said Kyle, laughing.

"Very funny," said Torie, trying not to laugh. "Now, will you start reading, please?"

"Okay, okay," said Kyle sheepishly. "I will, as soon as I finish my soda."

"No—now!" insisted Torie. "Or I'm sending *you* out to sea!"

With a grumble and a grimace, Kyle started reading again, for another five minutes. Then he started fiddling and fidgeting until he found another excuse to get up and move around.

It didn't take long for Torie to realize that she wouldn't be able to leave Kyle's side as long as they were studying. Without her standing over him, he wouldn't sit still. She wound up either reading every word along with him or else constantly watching him out of the corner of her eye. Still, by the time Torie and Kyle stopped studying, they had only covered the material Kyle was supposed to have studied in the first week of school, back in September!

"I think I've about had it," Kyle said, standing up and stretching. He reached his hand out to Torie and pulled her up to stand beside him.

"So was it as painful as you thought it would be?" Torie asked.

Kyle shook his head. "You know," he said, "you don't play fair, Torie. There's one thing you didn't warn me about."

"What's that?" Torie asked sleepily.

Kyle tilted her chin up toward him and kissed her gently on the lips. "Falling in love with the teacher, of course."

* * *

Almost a week later Torie had to admit that Kyle was doing his best. Torie really believed that. And his best was fairly impressive. Kyle was a fast learner, once he slowed down his body enough to sit still and read something. He'd covered about a month's schoolwork in almost a week.

Somewhere inside of him, Torie realized, Kyle must have wanted to study as much as she wanted him to. Otherwise, he simply wouldn't have gone through with it. Even though she knew that part of the reason he'd agreed to study was to see her, she was all-work during their study sessions—well, *almost* all-work.

From time to time, in the middle of reading or discussing something completely serious, Torie would find herself feeling awfully romantic. The sensation always came as a surprise—unexpected and irresistible. She'd find herself gazing at Kyle, wondering how any boy could be so good-looking, charming, and all-around wonderful. If her student was falling in love with his teacher, this teacher was definitely falling in love with her student. And that, Torie decided, was a very good thing because there were also drawbacks to working so hard with Kyle every night.

Naturally, the more time Torie spent working with Kyle, the less time she had for everything else in her life. She was barely keeping up with her own studies, squeezing them in before Kyle came or after he left. She hadn't seen Jo or Wendy outside of school in a week. She hadn't even looked at her writing since the day she had gone out to the farm. By the time Torie was done working with Kyle every night, she just wanted to flop into her bed.

Torie finally figured out that if she studied for her own finals right after school, she'd probably do all right. After all, she wasn't really behind in any of her classes.

Until the mail came on Tuesday, May 29. "There's a letter for you, hon," Torie's mother called from the kitchen as Torie was walking upstairs to her room. "Something from a publishing company."

Torie dropped her books and her purse on the steps and headed back downstairs. As casually as she could, she strolled into the kitchen and calmly glanced at the envelope on the counter. It was just what Torie hoped it would be: a letter from the publishing company she had sent her story to.

"What is it, hon?" asked Torie's mom.

"Who knows?" answered Torie, pretending to be uninterested. "Probably junk mail." But as she walked out of the kitchen, she read the return address on the envelope twice.

Torie had no intention of telling her mom or *anybody* that she had allowed Kyle to send her writing to a publishing company. The whole idea seemed so ridiculous, still, part of her was hoping.

Torie put her books and bag on her desk and kicked her bedroom door closed. Slowly, she sat down on the edge of her bed, took the letter out of the envelope, and read:

Dear Ms. Hilliard:

Thank you for submitting your manuscript to our company. Frankly, we rarely receive submissions from sixteen-year-old girls. However, we find your manuscript extremely interesting. Although we do not feel your work is ready for publication in its current form, we believe your writing has great merit.

I will be in the Arlenton area on June 5 and 6. If you can provide a complete, typed copy of your manuscript and deliver it to my room at the Arlenton Hotel on the evening of the fifth, I would be happy to read it and arrange a meeting on the sixth to discuss your work.

Please phone me with your response one week before June 5.

Sincerely,

Roberta Frenay

"Oh, my goodness," Torie said out loud and promptly read the letter over and over until she nearly had it memorized.

My writing has "great merit," she thought. *Fantastic!* She looked up "merit" in the dictionary, just in case the word had a few meanings she didn't know about.

Rolling over in bed, Torie reached across to her night table and picked up the phone to call Kyle. *No,* she decided, putting the phone back. *Not yet. I'll surprise him with the news when he comes over tonight.*

Instead, she read the letter again, then looked over at her calendar and sat up with a jolt. One week before June 5 meant that *day,* she realized. She had one hour to call the publisher before five o'clock.

Torie dropped the phone, as if it carried some contagious disease. She was downright scared to dial the phone and start talking with a real book publisher. This would require a little thought.

Popping up from her bed, Torie decided to go out for a brief walk to clear her head and to help her decide exactly what to say to Ms. Frenay. She headed downstairs. Then she turned around and went right back up. She was definitely too nervous to go for a walk.

Carrying the phone over to the other side of her room, she sat at her desk. *Now, this is better,* she thought. *It's more businesslike than my bed. Okay—here goes.* Torie dialed the telephone number printed on the publisher's letter. It rang. Torie twisted the phone cord around her fingers. The line kept ringing.

Torie started to calm down. She was thinking that maybe no one was in. Then she wouldn't have to talk.

"Roberta Frenay's office," came a voice finally.

"Hello," said Torie. "This is Tor—*Victoria* Hilliard."

"How may I help you?"

"I received a letter from Roberta Frenay," answered Torie.

"Are you a writer?"

The question startled Torie. She didn't feel she was qualified to call herself a "writer." Then again, it sounded wonderful. Torie couldn't quite get any answer out of her mouth.

"What's your name again, please?"

"Victoria Hilliard."

"Just a moment."

By now, Torie's nerves were as twisted as the phone cord around her fingers, and she hadn't even spoken to the right person yet!

When Ms. Frenay finally did get on the line, her tone was very professional but gentle and friendly. "Hello, Victoria. I'm so glad you called," she said. "How are you today?"

Torie settled down and relaxed. The next thing she knew, she was talking all about her writing. "I'm really glad you like my story," she said.

"It's more than a story," said Ms. Frenay. "I could see it as the initial phase of a full-fledged book."

"Someone else has told me that," responded Torie. "But I didn't believe him."

"Unfortunately, I have a significant concern," added Ms. Frenay. "I have to tell you that I haven't read about half of your manuscript."

"Really?" asked Torie. She was going to ask "why," but she thought that this might be the usual practice. Maybe every publisher only read half of a manuscript.

"You realize that your entire manuscript is written in longhand on lined paper. As a result, almost half of the photocopies you sent me are entirely illegible. Didn't you notice this when you made the copies?"

"Well, no," was all Torie could say. There was no point in blaming Kyle.

"That's why I needed to speak with you on the telephone," explained Ms. Frenay. "I want you to understand that I must be able to read your manuscript more thoroughly when we meet. Could you have a typed copy for me to review when I travel to Arlenton? If you deliver it to my hotel on June fifth, I'll have a chance to read it and will be ready to discuss it on June sixth."

Torie's voice rose an octave. "The whole thing—typed?"

"Yes, of course," Ms. Frenay said breezily. "It *is* standard practice. Otherwise, there's no point in—"

"Okay," said Torie.

"Good," the editor said. "I'll put you down for an appointment in Arlenton on June sixth. Someone from my office will call your home on the morning of the sixth to confirm. If you have any problems at that point, or if you're not prepared to meet with me, it's important that you let us know."

"If something goes wrong, can we make a different appointment?" Torie asked uncertainly.

There was a long moment's hesitation. "Well, as I said in my letter, submissions from sixteen-year-old girls are highly irregular," Ms. Frenay explained. "I'm looking forward to meeting you, but with my schedule, I—I suggest that you try your best to make this appointment, Victoria."

"I see," said Torie.

Chapter Twelve

One thing stuck in Torie's mind. Out of her entire conversation with the publishing company, she kept hearing one phrase over and over again: "Are you a writer?"

Fifteen minutes had passed since Torie spoke to Ms. Frenay, but she still hadn't gotten up from her desk chair. For some reason, staying in the same spot seemed to keep the excitement of the moment lingering.

Am I a writer? Torie asked herself.

Yes. It was true—a real book publisher was interested in Torie Hilliard's writing. They said her work had "great merit."

And it's all because of Kyle, Torie thought. *He's been right all along. That wild man's been absolutely right all along.*

There was still one problem, however. While

Torie was sitting at her desk, she started to do a little calculating. She needed to type her whole story, which was sixty-three pages long, and she had seven days to do it, including that night. At her top speed, without making a lot of mistakes, she could probably type one page in twenty minutes. That would be three pages per hour. Three divided into sixty-three is twenty-one, and that divided by seven days . . .

Torie had it all worked out. She would have to spend three hours a day typing. Then she could have her whole story finished in time to deliver to Ms. Frenay on June 5.

"Three hours a day!" Torie moaned aloud. With her schedule that week, she barely had enough time to eat and sleep. *Where am I ever going to find three more hours a day for typing?* she wondered.

Mentally tracing all her steps in the course of a day, Torie couldn't come up with very many options. The school day was obviously out of the question. After school, she did her homework. After dinner, when she helped Kyle, was the only time when she could type. There wasn't any other choice, and she knew that Kyle wouldn't mind. He'd be thrilled for her. She was certainly thrilled, and she owed it all to him.

But that particular night, Kyle wasn't in the mood to be thrilled about anything. In fact, he seemed depressed as he marched into the house without looking at her and headed straight for the chair in the rec room.

Torie sat down on the arm of the chair. "Kyle," she asked gently, "what's the matter?"

"Nothing. I'm fine," said Kyle.

Not when your voice sounds like that, Torie thought.

"How are you doing?" he asked in the same flat tone.

For now, Torie thought, it might be best to wait a little while before she told Kyle her news. Her main concern at the moment was *him.* "Oh, I'm fine," she answered. "Are you sure *you're* okay?"

"Yeah," he said. But Torie knew better. She could sense the tension written across his face.

"Kyle, please—you can tell me. What's on your mind?"

Kyle just stared at the carpet as if it were the most fascinating thing he'd ever seen.

Torie tried another approach. "Okay, then," she said, standing up. "Let's get to work. Now, yesterday we—"

"What's the use?" Kyle muttered under his breath.

"I heard that," Torie said.

"Well, it's true," said Kyle. "There's no point to all this anymore. It's not helping me."

"Of course it is," said Torie, getting up to stand in front of him.

"Sure, sure," Kyle answered sarcastically. "It didn't do me any good today."

"What happened today? Did you have a test or something?"

"Yeah, in history," answered Kyle. "On World War Two."

"World War Two? But we're only up to the Civil War," said Torie.

"I know," said Kyle. "But the rest of the class is up to World War Two."

"Oh, boy." Torie sighed. She sat back down on the arm of Kyle's chair. "I'll tell you one thing, you are *wrong*. How can you say that all our studying hasn't done anything—that it hasn't helped you? Just look at you!" she continued. "There's the proof right there. Look at how upset you are—because you flunked a test. Now tell me something: When in your life were you ever upset because you flunked a test? Never!"

"That much is true," Kyle admitted.

"You're starting to care now, Kyle. And that's pretty important."

Kyle looked straight at Torie and seemed to

brighten up. "You know, Tor, it's all because of you."

"And you," she said. "You're the one who's been willing to change." She grinned at him. "Now let's not get too sentimental here. We've got a lot of work to do tonight. We still think Abraham Lincoln's the President, and Franklin D. Roosevelt's here already."

Studying harder and longer than ever, Torie and Kyle covered eighty years of Mexican history in four hours flat. The night was so intense that Torie had hardly thought about the three hours of typing she had planned to do. As for telling Kyle all about it, the last thing Torie would have done then was tell Kyle that she couldn't help him anymore. Unfortunately, Torie only had six days left to type her manuscript. And to catch up on the schedule she had worked out, she would have to type for *six* hours on Wednesday.

When Kyle came over on Wednesday night, Torie wasn't sure how to handle the whole situation. So she still didn't tell him anything about it. She didn't know what to say.

If she told Kyle everything, he would insist on going home so she could type and then, she was sure all their hard work would be wasted. Kyle worked hard, but he wouldn't work without her.

Torie decided then and there that she simply wouldn't tell him. But her heart sank when she realized what that meant—she wouldn't be able to get her manuscript typed, and she'd have to cancel her appointment with Ms. Frenay. It was painful, but she knew how important it was that Kyle pass his finals.

So she worked harder and harder with Kyle every night. By the time they were through on Thursday, he was ready for his math final. By Friday night, he was ready for science. So far, so good.

On Saturday, they were planning to work on history. The last day, Sunday, was going to be special. Torie named it R & R Day, for Review & Reward. She and Kyle planned to go over all of Kyle's material one last time. Then, if he really knew his stuff, they would celebrate and go out for the first time in two weeks.

On Saturday morning Torie woke up feeling as if she was coming down the home stretch. Kyle was doing better than she had dared hope, and she even felt all right about her own exams. There was just one more thing she wanted to do during the weekend. Before Kyle came over that night, she had a letter to write—to Roberta Frenay. Although

Torie was planning to phone her to cancel their appointment before Ms. Frenay showed up, she still wanted to explain the whole situation in depth.

She put it off all day, but finally, just after noon, she sat down at her desk. Usually, Torie was good with words, but this letter was one of the most difficult things she'd ever have to write. She couldn't quite explain her situation, no matter how she phrased it. Somehow either she or Kyle always came out sounding like a silly kid. Torie didn't expect the letter to take more than an hour to write. But she wrote and crumpled up letters and kept on writing and crumpling till midafternoon.

Finally she settled on a draft that sounded awkward, but did explain everything Ms. Frenay needed to know. Then Torie moved over to her bed, lay down, and read it again and again.

"Torie, Kyle's here," her mother suddenly shouted from downstairs.

What? Torie thought, checking her clock. It was four o'clock already. "Coming!" she shouted back. Hurrying, she changed her top, shoved the letter under her pillow where nobody would find it, and put Ms. Frenay's letter in the big envelope where she always kept her manuscript. Quickly, she tucked the envelope on a shelf and went downstairs.

This was the earliest Torie and Kyle had ever started working together, and Torie was amazed at how hard Kyle worked.

"Slow down," she said as he began rattling off the major figures in the Korean War. "I can barely keep up with you."

Kyle grinned at her. "Don't worry about it. I know a very patient teacher. He lives on a horse farm about ten miles north of here . . ."

Torie threw a pillow at him, and they went back to work.

By eight that evening both of them were exhausted, but their work was paying off. Kyle was just about ready for his exams.

"Ask me anything," he said, sitting on the floor in front of the couch. "Go ahead."

"All right," said Torie. She was lying down on the couch, behind him. "What makes you so cocky?"

"Come on, I've got all this stuff down— thanks to you," he said with a grin. "You know what, Tor? We should *really* celebrate. Let's do something extra-special tomorrow, before the school week starts. You want to go to the summer auction with me?"

"No—and you're not going, either, remember?" said Torie, sternly.

"Come on, I'm as ready for these exams as I'll ever be."

"I doubt it," said Torie. "I'm not even ready. Now that you're so brilliant, you should come over and help *me* tomorrow."

"I can't do any more, Tor. If you've got some work to do, you may as well do it now," said Kyle. "I'm going to catch up on my history. Let's see if there's a war movie on TV." He clicked on the remote control and flipped through the channels.

"Okay, hand me my science text," said Torie.

Within an hour, Kyle was engrossed in a movie on TV, and Torie was fast asleep with her chemistry book on her stomach.

When he saw that she was fast asleep, Kyle gently took the chemistry book away and tiptoed out of the rec room. Quietly, he went up to her room to look for a pillow and a blanket. Torie didn't hear him when he returned to the rec room fifteen minutes later and gently covered her with a soft quilt. She didn't know that Kyle watched her sleep for a while and then quietly let himself out the front door.

Chapter Thirteen

"Torie, wake up, hon."

"Huh?" Torie couldn't quite focus, but she realized her mother was shaking her gently.

"It's after midnight. You fell asleep in the rec room. I think Kyle must have brought down the pillow and blanket. Now, come on, it's time you went upstairs."

Torie tried to say something coherent, but her head hurt, and despite the blanket, she was chilled. Groggy and aching, she stumbled up to her room, undressed quickly, and fell into bed. "Oh, no," Torie mumbled as she felt the letter she wrote to Ms. Frenay crumpled under her pillow.

Flipping on the lamp on her night table, Torie crawled back out of bed. She swung over to her desk to put the letter in the envelope with her manuscript. "Where *is* that envelope?" she muttered. But the light hurt her eyes, and she was so sleepy that she couldn't even think about looking for the envelope. Instead, she simply threw the letter away, turned off the light, and fell fast asleep again.

When she woke up for good on Sunday morning, Torie still felt groggy. It was late—past eleven—and she always felt a little funny after she overslept. Getting up and walking around in the middle of the night hadn't helped, either.

Whatever the reasons, Torie had an uncomfortable feeling all through Sunday. Everything around her took on a strange quality. Her parents' voices sounded a little louder, and the lights in the house seemed brighter. *I hope I'm not getting sick,* she thought. She wished Kyle had woken her up the night before so she could have gotten a normal night's sleep in her own bed. She didn't understand why he had simply disappeared, without even saying good night.

Right after dinner. Torie went into the rec room and started her own studying, so she could get as much done as possible before Kyle came over. The reading gave her a little headache, but she stuck with it. The longer she read, the more she got absorbed in her books, and by the time she finally stopped, Torie was surprised at herself. She had finished her own studying, and Kyle hadn't even arrived.

She checked her watch to see how much longer she had until Kyle was supposed to show up. She had been so involved in her reading that she didn't realize how much time had passed. It was eight o'clock, which meant that Kyle was already late—*two hours* late.

This isn't like Kyle at all, Torie thought. *He's never been more than a few minutes late. And he wouldn't miss our date tonight, not when we're actually going to go out for the first time in two weeks.* The more Torie thought about it, the worse her headache got. But she decided to give Kyle the benefit of the doubt, and wait.

And wait. By nine o'clock, Torie had waited long enough. She was furious, and her head was pounding. She was worried, too—she hoped Kyle hadn't gotten into some sort of trouble or an accident. Then again, as long as he was all right, *she* wanted to kill him.

She grabbed the extension line in the rec room and dialed Kyle's number. It rang and rang for some time, but no one answered.

That's funny, she thought. *Nobody's home. Not even Kyle's parents. I wonder where . . .*

Suddenly it hit her. *The auction!* Obviously, Kyle had gone to the summer auction. She'd spent all that time working with him, and even given up her chance to have her story published, and he skipped out on the night that meant the most to her. She was angry, and she felt like a total fool. Obviously, he hadn't changed at all. Kyle Fontana still did whatever he wanted to.

Torie set the phone down in a daze, and then slowly made her way to her room. Very deliberately, she walked over to her bedroom windows and yanked the curtains closed. She never wanted to see the Fontana farm again.

Her head was on fire, and her whole body hurt, but even worse was the way she felt inside. Torie had never been hurt like this before. She lay down on the bed and cried until she cried herself to sleep.

On Monday morning Torie felt a little better—physically, that is. Her headache was gone, but the ache in her heart got worse the more she thought about Kyle.

Since her final exams began that day, she resolved that she simply wouldn't think about Kyle, which was easier said than done. *At least I won't look for him,* she told herself as she walked toward Spanish class. *And if I do happen to see him, I'm going to stay cool,* she vowed, *icy, freezing cool.*

As it turned out, Torie didn't see Kyle at all. She stayed cool, all right, but it began to take quite a bit of effort to stay that way. She thought about him all through her history exam, and halfway into the day, she started sort of seeing if she might notice him, out of the corner of her eye. But there was no sign of Kyle anywhere all day.

Finally, on her way out of her last class, Torie strolled by the administrative offices and checked the daily absentee listing. Because exams had begun that day, the list was practically empty, with the exception of some very ill kids, some total losers, and one Kyle Fontana.

Torie's eyes widened in disbelief. *Kyle hadn't even come to school!* He stayed out late at the auction, then didn't even bother to get up and come to school today, Torie told herself. Obviously, all that work and sacrifice had been for nothing. Standing there, numb, Torie drew a total blank. She couldn't think.

But her head cleared up as she headed back toward her homeroom where the time of her math exam was going to be posted. Kyle was walking straight toward her.

He was a weird and horrible sight. His clothes were rumpled, his hair was uncombed, he hadn't shaved—in fact, he looked as if he hadn't even showered lately.

He walked toward Torie and stopped alongside her. She wanted to keep on walking past him. Yet she couldn't.

"Well, your big auction was last night," Torie said. "Did you stay out late?"

"I'm sorry I didn't come over," Kyle answered.

"You could have called," said Torie.

"I forgot," said Kyle. "I guess I was just too wrapped up."

"You *forgot*?" said Torie. "Obviously, I don't understand how wonderful the great auction is. But it must mean a lot more to you than I do." She tried to keep her voice down, since she and Kyle were standing in the middle of the hallway, with the rest of Arlenton High School walking all around them. She was rapidly losing her temper, though.

"I'm sorry you were too wrapped up with whatever you were doing," she went on. "But it all must have been so much more important than our date! Is that right?"

Torie could see fire flaring up in Kyle's eyes.

"Hey—maybe it was! Don't push me, Torie," he said dangerously.

"What? Don't push *you*?" she demanded indignantly. "Don't you know how you've hurt me? Don't you understand?"

"Maybe you don't understand me," said Kyle.

"You're right. I don't." Torie's voice was rising to a furious pitch. "I *don't* understand you. And I never will. You know why? Because I think you're selfish and inconsiderate. You do exactly what you want to do without a thought for anyone else. And I think I've wasted more than enough time on you. I'm sorry, but that's the way I feel. As far as I'm concerned, I don't care if—"

Kyle turned his back on Torie and walked away.

Still shaking with anger, Torie watched him go, then stormed off to her homeroom. Fortunately, the room was empty. Torie was so upset that she didn't want to see anyone. She quickly checked the time of her exam, ran over to her desk, grabbed the envelope she kept her writing in, and started out of the room to go home. Then she stopped short.

"I didn't leave this envelope in there," Torie said aloud. "I didn't even bring it to school."

Slowly Torie sat down at the desk closest to her and opened up the envelope. She pulled out the thick stack of papers and held it in her two hands, her eyes wide with disbelief. There was her manuscript—*completely typed*.

A note was clipped to the top page:

Dear Torie,

I accidentally found the letter you wrote to the publisher. All I can say is thank you.

And I love you very much.

Kyle.

P.S. Sorry this took me so long, but I'm a lousy typer and my mom's typewriter stinks.

Chapter Fourteen

For a moment Torie just sat there staring at Kyle's note. She couldn't believe what he'd just done for her—or what she'd just said to him.

Quickly Torie stuffed the papers back into the envelope and ran down the hallway. She kept running until she reached the middle of the sidewalk right outside the main school entrance. Kids streaming out of the building bumped into her from both sides, but Torie barely noticed. She stood stiff and still, staring across the school grounds.

Finally, squinting into the distance, she spotted Kyle in the student parking lot. He was heading toward his Jeep.

Okay, Torie Hilliard, she told herself. *You know what to do.*

She made it to the sidewalk by the parking lot a minute before Kyle was about to pull out. Torie took a deep breath. Then as Kyle drove up the driveway out of the parking lot, Torie deliberately walked straight across the driveway, paying no attention to the Jeep. Kyle's brakes screeched. Torie's envelope fell to the ground an inch from Kyle's wheels.

"Torie!" Kyle shouted. He climbed out of his Jeep, his eyes on fire. "What in the world are you doing? Didn't you see me coming?"

He bent down and picked up Torie's envelope, then quickly pulled out the papers and flipped through them all. "Good—they're all right," he said with a sigh of relief. Then he turned on her, outraged. "You could have ruined all my work," he said. "You know how long it took me to type this stuff?"

"Kyle," said Torie nervously, "I have to tell you something."

"What's that?" asked Kyle angrily. "You've already told me quite a bit."

"But not everything," said Torie. "There's one more thing."

Kyle just stood there and stared her down.

Torie felt so emotional that she was almost shaking. She could barely get out the words. "Kyle," she said in a weak, shaky voice. "I love you very much, too."

Kyle gave her a long, searching look, then his expression softened, and the fire in his eyes died down. He reached toward Torie and took her in his arms. "I'm so sorry, Tor," he whispered, his mouth pressed to the top of her head.

"Me, too, Kyle. I can't tell you how sorry I am. I never should have said those things—or even thought them." As the two of them squeezed each other tightly, car horns started honking all around them. "Maybe we'd better get in the Jeep, though," said Torie with a smile. "I think we're causing a traffic jam."

"Kyle, there's still one thing that upsets me, though," said Torie as they drove toward her house. "You missed your history exam today. Now you're going to flunk the course. After all that studying, you didn't even get to take the exam."

"Shows what you know, goody-goody girl," said Kyle. "I can tell that you never missed an exam. Listen, I couldn't get out of taking that exam if I wanted to. As soon as I walk in class tomorrow morning, they're going to throw a make-up exam at me." He stopped at a traffic light and grinned at her. "And I'll be ready for it," he said. "You know, Tor, I owe it all to you."

"Well, I've got a big day coming up, too,"

said Torie, looking down at her manuscript. She wriggled over next to Kyle, curled up alongside him, and held the thick stack of pages in her hands. "I just can't get over that you really did this for me, Kyle."

Smiling, Torie started to flip through the manuscript. "I only hope all your work was worth it," she murmured. "I really don't know if this is any good."

"*I* do," said Kyle as he put his arm around her.

Torie set her manuscript down on the seat and put her head on Kyle's shoulder. "I'll deliver it tomorrow, and we'll know for sure on Wednesday," she said, closing her eyes.

Torie had just finished her breakfast on Wednesday when the phone rang. "I'll get it," she called to her parents.

"Victoria, this is Roberta Frenay. I was wondering if it would be possible to meet at your house at ten this morning. Of course, I'll call your school and arrange permission for you. I'm sure it won't take more than a couple of hours."

"Uh, sure," said Torie. "That would be fine."

"Good, I'm looking forward to meeting you."

Then before Torie even had the presence of mind to say good-bye, the conversation was over.

Torie hung up the phone and immediately picked it up again and dialed Kyle's number.

"Hi, Tor," he answered. "What's the word?"

"Ten o'clock," she replied. "Ms. Frenay's coming here at ten. She said we should be finished by noon, so I can get back to school. I don't have any exams this morning, so it should be okay. Can you come and pick me up at lunchtime?"

"Absolutely not," said Kyle teasingly. "I'm not going to allow a successful writer like you to ride in a Jeep. After this morning, it's strictly *limos* for you."

"I knew I called you too early in the morning. You're still *dreaming*!" said Torie. "Just be here—okay?"

"Of course," said Kyle. "And, Tor—good luck."

"Thanks," said Torie. "I'm going to need it!"

Talking to Kyle made Torie feel a little bit better, but she was still very nervous about meeting Ms. Frenay. Unfortunately, there wasn't anything for her to do about her nerves except simply hang tough until ten o'clock.

When Ms. Frenay arrived she immediately put Torie at ease. First of all, she looked younger than Torie had pictured her. And though she was businesslike, she was also surprisingly warm and friendly.

After chatting about the weather and Ms. Frenay's journey for a few minutes, Torie led the editor into the living room.

"Would you like some coffee or tea?" Torie asked nervously.

"No, thank you. I hope you don't mind, Victoria, but I'm afraid I'm on a terribly tight schedule today," Ms. Frenay explained.

Ms. Frenay pulled Torie's manuscript out of her briefcase and set it on the coffee table between them. She didn't say anything for a long moment.

Torie stared at her story, unable to meet Ms. Frenay's eyes. *She hates it,* Torie decided, *and she's trying to find a polite way to tell me so.*

"Victoria," Ms. Frenay said, folding her hands in front of her, "I love it!"

Torie almost jumped up from her seat. But she tried her best to stay cool. "Really?" she said.

"Really," said Ms Frenay with a nod and a broad smile. "This book is genuinely excellent. It has something very special. It has *heart*, and that's something no one can fake."

Torie was afraid she might break down and cry with happiness.

"Now, I am not saying that this is a perfect manuscript," continued Ms. Frenay. "On the contrary, it still needs work—quite a bit of work, as a matter of fact. But I don't want us to dwell on the negatives at this particular point. Our editors can work very closely with you, after we sign a publishing contract."

"A *contract*?" said Torie. She could barely believe her ears. "You mean you want to *buy* my book!"

"We'll have to work out the details with your parents, since you're a minor, which we should probably do in our offices in New York."

Suddenly the doorbell rang. It took Torie by surprise, since Kyle wasn't due to pick her up for another hour.

"Excuse me," said Torie. She walked out of the living room into the hall, where she could see Kyle through the front-door glass.

She was so excited that she couldn't hide her feelings when she and Kyle looked into each other's eyes.

"I knew it!" hooted Kyle from the other side of the door.

Torie opened the door a crack, so as to not make a scene in front of Ms. Frenay. "Sssshhh," she said, trying not to laugh. "What are you doing here already? I thought I told you to pick me up at noon."

"I couldn't wait," said Kyle through the crack in the door. "Besides, I got done early."

"Got done with what?"

"My history exam."

"Oh, my goodness!" said Torie. "I almost forgot all about it. What happened? How did you do?" But she didn't really have to ask. The answer was written all over Kyle's face. He looked as if he were going to burst with pride.

Torie swung the front door wide open, and she held on to Kyle as tightly as she could. "Oh, Kyle, I'm so proud of you," she said. Tears were streaming down her face.

Then, remembering about Ms. Frenay, Torie pulled herself away from Kyle and dried her eyes with her sleeves. She took Kyle by the hand and began to lead him into the living room.

But Ms. Frenay, on her way out of the living room, was already walking right toward them.

"I'm very glad to have helped you have such a happy day, Victoria," she said with a slight smile.

"I'd like to introduce you to Kyle Fontana, Ms. Frenay," said Torie. "Kyle, this is Ms. Frenay."

"Hi," he said, and he and Ms. Frenay shook hands.

"We'll be in touch with you very soon, Victoria," she said as she was leaving. "In the meantime, you might want to start thinking about one thing. You're going to need a title for your book, you know.

"Also," she added, "it would be a very good idea to practice your typing. It's not nearly as good as your writing."

Torie and Kyle burst out laughing as they closed the door behind Ms. Frenay. "Well, you did it," said Kyle, holding Torie by the waist. "All you need now is a title."

"Thanks," said Torie. "Have any ideas?"

"I only have one idea right now," said Kyle. "But there aren't any words for it."

"Oh, yeah?" said Torie teasingly. "And what's your big idea?"

"This—" said Kyle. He took Torie tightly in his arms. And Kyle gave Torie a long, sweet kiss she would never forget for the rest of her life.